DRAGON NIGHTS

NOTES OF NECROSOPH

AL K. LINE

Copyright © 2021 Al K. Line

The Boy Does Nothing

"Those fucking ubermarkets!" shouted Phage as she slammed the front door.

I heaved out of my lovely, stinky brown recliner with utmost haste, picked up an ornament I swear I'd never seen before, and began rubbing it with my sleeve. A man's got to look busy.

"What are you doing?" she asked suspiciously, as I stood there, eyes darting, panicked.

"Um... Dusting?"

"With your sleeve?"

"Maybe. Er, yeah, maybe I was. You got a problem with that?"

"No, you carry right on *dusting* with your sleeve," she laughed, eyes sparkling in the way that made me love her more each day. "While you're at it, why don't you hoover the murder rug with your big, fat, lying mouth!" Phage grinned devilishly and delightfully, then frowned as she remembered she was in a foul mood and needed to vent. "Where was I?"

"Stupid fucking ubermarkets?" I offered.

"Yeah. What the hell is with those places? It's bad enough they're now only open for a few hours, and there are more bloody self-service checkouts than food aisles, but now they're playing bloody Milli Vanilli? What gives?"

"Everyone began to enjoy the death metal. It was meant to make people hurry and do their shopping without hanging about, but it ended up doing the opposite. Sales of Corrosion of Conformity, Napalm Death, and Extreme Noise Terror went through the roof. Apparently, Milli Vanilli's record company did a massive deal with a few ubermarkets to see if it would work for them."

"Did it?"

"Nope."

"Good." Phage stormed off into the kitchen; I stared at my chair longingly. I was having such a lovely snooze too.

Being the perfect husband that I undoubtedly was, I nipped out of the front door and grabbed the rest of the shopping. I carried it through to the kitchen where Phage was staring into space, a bent carrot in one hand, a comedy turnip in the other.

"What you gonna do with those?" I asked, suddenly very afraid.

"Don't even ask."

"What's up?"

Phage dropped the "real" vegetables and flung herself at me, sobbing her heart out.

"Hey, hey, what's the matter? I know Milli Vanilli aren't everyone's cup of tea, but each to their own. It wasn't that bad, was it?"

"It's not that," she sighed, wiping at her eyes. "It's everything. Nothing's normal any more. Not that it's ever been. But I mean everything else, apart from the usual."

"I know. I know. It's getting weirder out there by the minute. Can't believe they've totally scrapped the electric car thing. It seemed like we were finally going to get some proper transport. Bloody REEs."

"Soph, what are you even saying? What's REEs? And I didn't mean cars. That's the last thing I was worrying about."

I wondered if I should resume my dusting. Maybe my dozing?

"Sorry. Rare Earth Elements. That's what they're called, and there aren't enough. That's why there's hardly any batteries. They can't do the car thing." Phage scowled at me. "Come on, tell me what happened."

"I fell off my bike. A man shouted at me because I was putting sunscreen on like they said we should, even in the bloody winter, and he hadn't had his quota. Nobody smiled in the ubermarket. The prices were ridiculous. There's no beef. No cheese. There's no cheese, Soph! Cheese! We need cheese!" Phage burst into tears again. I wrapped her in my arms and put my face into her hair. She smelled lovely. Of peach and apple and home. Of sanctuary.

"We do love cheese," I said softly.

She pulled away after a while and sniffed then smiled. "Sorry. I'm being silly. But this morning, with the bloody note, I wanted to do something nice for us both now you're home and up and about. It all went wrong."

"I've got everything I need right here," I told her. "You and Jen. That's all I need. Screw the cheese!" I shouted, grinning at my wife of twenty years.

"Yes. Fuck it!" she yelled, looking slightly manic.

The note on the table squirmed. Our combined mood took an instant downward spiral.

"We should open it, you know," I told her.

"I can't. I just can't bear it. Why is this happening to us? What's the point? You got out of hospital yesterday. You're not well."

"I'm fine. I did seven push-ups. I'm a little weak, and my side hurts a bit, but I'm all fixed. Come on, we can do this. We have to do this." I took her gently by the shoulders, turned her to face me, and told her, "We have to do this. Yes, I want to cry, yes, I am not at my best, and yes, I wanted to take it easy. I can't stand this either, and I came close to breaking this time, but we have to."

"You're so brave. How can you go on? How can you stand it?"

"I can't stand it. It's driving me mental, but we have no choice. We never have, we never will. Look, I know it sounds weird, but I actually feel better about this note than any other."

"Why?"

I held my wife's gaze, stared into beautiful, dark hazel eyes, and I told her the truth from the bottom of my heart. "Because I love you and I worry every time you go out the door. I can't bear it when you leave because of your note. This time, I can be there with you. I can help. I know you don't need protecting, hell, I've got the scars to prove I'm worse at this than you, but still. I want to look after you. You and Jen. So, yeah, there. I said it."

"My handsome, brave man. I love you."

"I love you too. Now, make my bloody dinner, woman. I'm starving. Don't you know I just got out of the hospital?"

The note squirmed again, forgotten for a moment. Phage snatched it up before anything demonic happened, and with a nod from me, she unfolded the despicable piece of paper.

"Salty. Newt."

"Fucking app," I complained, and not for the first time.

"I own this table," droned Mr. Wonderful, our annoying, smarmy, immortal cat as he sauntered across the scrubbed pine, blatantly ignoring us because we weren't him. "I own these humans. I own the stupid dog. I own those funny vegetables. They're mine. I own the land. I own the—"

"Get off the bloody table," we shouted in unison.

"The table is mine," he droned on, utterly ignoring us, not even bothering to look our way as he reached the edge, peered over the side, then flowed like water onto the chair. "I own this chair..." On and on he blathered as he wandered from the kitchen into the hallway. The catflap banged open then closed. All was silent.

6

"Idiot cat," I mumbled.

"I like him." Phage grinned. She picked up her phone from the counter, removed the protective case, and reluctantly typed the words into the Necroapp.

"He hates you. Mr. Wonderful would eat your eyeballs and complain they weren't salty enough. He's evil in cute fluffy cat form. What's the app say? Is it working? Damn thing always keeps me waiting. That bloody wheel going around and around."

"It's working. It's already done. Look."

"Do I have to?" Phage nodded, the mood serious. I pulled out my glasses then studied the phone. "Ugh, that's a rough route. It's gonna be a hassle getting there with the snow if it keeps falling."

"Knowing the weather we've been getting, it'll be sunny and scorching hot tomorrow."

"Yeah, maybe. You up for this?"

"Not really, no. And I know you aren't. You need rest."

"Guess I'll rest when I'm dead. But look, I've had months doing nothing, so I've had as much down time as I can stomach. I'll be fine. It's you I'm worried about."

"Me?"

"Yes. And me, actually. We're doing this together, and it worries me. We've never, you know, killed anyone with the other there. I don't want you to see me like that."

"And neither do I. Let's make a pact."

"A pact?"

"What we do out there, when we fulfill the Necronote, that's different people. This is us here, at home. A family. Out there, it's like being soldiers. We mustn't hold back because of each other. That way we could both die. So, a pact. Family at home, soldiers on the road. Deal?"

"Deal." I kissed my wife hard. "Are soldiers allowed to kiss when on duty?"

"They better be, or I'm going to be breaking a lot of rules."

Hand in hand, we went upstairs to break a few more.

"Come on, let's go and meet Jen from school. I miss that," I told Phage. She stared at me funny. "What? I do."

"Men," she sighed.

"What does that mean?"

"How many times have you gone to pick her up?"

"Gosh. Let me see?" I did some mental arithmetic. "Loads?" I ventured nervously.

"Seven. In all the years she's been in school, you've picked her up seven times. And that's including the times I came with you. Which is five."

"Shut up! Haha, you are such a kidder. Come on, let's go meet her. She's probably nearly home by now."

Phage gave me a look; it reminded me of how Mr. Wonderful glared at me. It wasn't seven, was it?

Jen was of an age now where she didn't need, or want, her parents picking her up from the local village school. She could ride her bike, chat to friends, that kind of thing. But once more wouldn't hurt.

We locked up the house, hopped on our bikes, then free-wheeled along quiet lanes. It was nice. I hadn't ridden for months, and needed the exercise. We'd be doing a lot of it over the next few days, so I guess I should get in what practice I could. It was also amazing to be outside in the country again after being cooped up in a sterile room. I missed this place so much.

The snow had melted off the road, but it was wet, and there were several patches of ice you had to watch out for. Should Jen have ridden to school in this? She was sensible and Phage had told her to push it if she felt it unsafe, and besides, Jen was tough. And wore her helmet.

We got halfway down the lane and spied Jen puffing and panting as she pedaled towards us. Her frosty breath made her look like Tyr, our very own dragon. She saw us and waved, smiling. We waved back and pulled over to the verge to wait.

The screeching of tires made me turn in time to see a beat-up Subaru belching smoke come skidding along the road, weaving all over the place. As he passed us, I saw the fear on the driver's sweaty face. Time slowed as I turned in Jen's direction and screamed, "Jump into the hedge. Now!"

Jen looked up, saw the out-of-control car, and panicked. She pedaled hard, tried to get off the road and onto the strip of grass, but caught her wheel in the ditch and the bike skidded sideways. She toppled off, the bike flew into the hedge, and Jen slid across the road.

The Subaru weaved desperately, then bounced right over my daughter. The driver regained control then the bastard sped up and was gone.

My insides went cold. Phage screamed. I knew this was it. My worst nightmare had come to pass.

We ran, numb with shock, down the road, falling repeatedly, until finally we skidded to a halt where Jen lay.

"No, no, no," I wailed.

Phage knelt, and cradled the broken body of our daughter, rocked her back and forth, howling as the tears fell freely.

Jen's body was ruined. Her arm was bent the wrong way, the shin bone stuck out of her leg, jagged and bloodied, and there were tire tracks over her school jumper.

She wasn't breathing.

I didn't know what to do. I didn't know if I'd ever do anything again. I could not lose another child. I simply couldn't.

My brain refused to function. My body refused to act. I was helpless. What should I do?

And then Jen gasped, as though trying to inhale the world. She coughed and her eyes snapped open. I breathed for what felt like the first time. I cried for joy that she was alive, as she had definitely been dead.

Phage laughed manically and asked, "Are you okay? I mean apart from the leg and the arm? Does it hurt? Oh, honey, we thought we'd lost you."

"I'm... I'm okay. He ran me over. Unbelievable. Can I get up now?"

"You have to stay still," I told her. "Don't move. There could be internal bleeding."

"No, I'm fine. My bum hurts where I bumped it, but I'm okay. What was that about my arm and leg?" Jen looked at her leg and frowned. Then at her arm, still bent the wrong way. She closed her eyes, seemingly unconcerned, and I felt the whispers surround us. Whispers, words of the witches, sometimes to help begin healing, other times to destroy. But Jen was eleven, and hadn't even begun to learn of such things. And yet, somehow she knew.

The sisters. The damn line of crones that stretched back to the beginning on Phage's side. The knowledge inherited by the most powerful, after long years of training. We'd seen a glimpse of it years ago when Jen named Kayin, but nothing much since.

It was clear she'd been keeping secrets. I knew why. Pethach, that bitch witch. But if it saved my daughter...

The whispers sharpened, their power growing, until I couldn't think, could hardly see, as the magic enveloped me and held me tight like a glove. And then it was gone, and the world was quiet.

Jen's leg was fixed. The protruding bone was back where it belonged and the wound was already sealed. Red and angry, but closed tighter than a dwarf's purse. The arm was moving freely, and my darling daughter was on her feet, smiling, as she rubbed at her sore bottom.

"Is my bike okay?" she asked. Jen held out her hands to help her parents up from the middle of the road on a freezing winter's day when they believed their daughter was dead.

Confused, still terrified, and more worried about my daughter than I'd ever been in my entire life, I scrambled to my feet and helped Phage up, who was glassy-eyed, pale, and sweating. We both gawped at Jen.

"What? Come on, it's freezing out here. Dad, will you push my bike? I feel kinda funny." Jen smiled weakly at me, then began walking up the lane.

We watched her go, but then she faltered as her leg buckled. I heard the snap as the bone that moments ago was healed prodded back through the leg. Her arm twisted unnaturally and Jen screamed as it bent the wrong way. She collapsed onto the icy ground.

We ran to her. I warned Phage to be careful, but it was clear she was out cold. Jen may have the power of the entire sisterhood behind her, but even they couldn't just heal snapped bones in seconds. Jen's recovery was short-lived, but she had the gifts of the witches, that was undeniable.

I scooped her up as I silently repeated the registration of the Subaru.

We walked in silence to the gate, bikes forgotten. As Phage fumbled with the latch, a familiar shifting of the air caused me to turn.

"Hello Pethach," I sighed.

"Soph," she nodded, gasping as she bent double, raven hair covering her face for a moment, hiding the anguish of morphing such a distance.

Great, this was just great. Injured daughter and now my bitch witch mother-in-law.

Talk about being thrown back in at the deep end. My first day home and not only was there a Necronote, but my daughter had nearly been killed, and my mother-in-law had apparently come to stay.

I should have stayed in the hospital.

Home, Sick, Blue

"Mother," gasped Phage, "what are you doing here? And how did you morph so far?" Phage got the gate open, then unlocked the front door. I carried Jen inside as mother and daughter followed.

"I have been practicing," said Peth from behind me.

"Yeah, I bet," I grunted.

"And what does that mean?" hissed the bitch witch as I moved into the living room and put the still-unconscious Jen on my recliner. I unfastened her helmet and tried not to move her body more than was necessary. It didn't look good at all.

Knowing I would soon forget, and I really didn't want to, I grabbed a pen and pad from the side table and scribbled the registration down, then turned to the two women.

Phage was beside Jen, checking her over. Peth stood, stoic in all her powerful glory, but I saw the pain she endured, the clenched jaw, the sheen of sweat. She'd morphed from the witch enclave to here the moment she felt an issue with Jen, that was clear, but traveling this far was a strain, even for one such as her. She'd been practicing alright, and it was because four years ago I'd morphed further than any witch and a lot faster too. She was shocked and would no doubt have been training to ensure no man ever got the better of the witches. That was her way, her attitude. The sisters, the women she called sisters, were funny about men being involved in the Necroverse at all. Especially family.

"I asked you a question," said Peth, staring at me with her weird horizontal slit pupils, designed to increase her peripheral vision but really there just to make others squirm.

"It means you wanted to be as good as me at morphing." I glared back at her, not in the mood for this shit.

"Nonsense." She waved it away. "It was for such an emergency as this."

"Didn't see you come rushing when I was at death's door. Or when Phage gets hurt."

"You are adults, and my services were not required and would have made no difference."

"Whatever." I turned to Phage. "Okay, what do we do? This is your call. Should I phone for an ambulance?"

Phage looked down at Jen. Her chest was rising and falling slowly, her body relaxed. Undoubtedly, she was in shock, and badly hurt, but I knew the witches, especially Peth, were old hands at repairing broken bones with their whispers. Phage was good at it too, but she wasn't anywhere near as accomplished as her mother.

"No!" said Peth. "We can fix her. She's better off at home."

"That's not your call, Mother," snapped Phage with a serious scowl. "You don't even know what happened."

"I assume she got run over." Peth shrugged. "We can fix her."

"You haven't even looked at her properly," I told Peth. "None of us have. You don't know what the internal injuries are. What about her head? Right, I'm calling the doctor."

"No, wait," said Phage. She frowned, unsure what to do. This was our daughter, but she wasn't like other girls, and the last thing we needed was for Jen to do something that would draw attention to our family. I read all that because I felt the same way. But still, it was our little girl and my heart was breaking.

"You sure?" I asked.

Phage nodded. "Let me check her over. Let us check her. If it's just broken bones, Mother and I can fix her. If there is any internal injury then we call an ambulance. Hurry, Mother, we must be sure. And fast."

Peth walked forward regally. Her loose white blouse and silk trousers wafted perfume my way. She wasn't your average-looking witch, that was for sure. She wasn't dressed for the weather, either.

I chewed the skin from my knuckles while they bent to Jen and the whispers began. Almost silent words of exploration and healing. Their learned spells, their magic, their summoning of unknowable-to-me energies wrapped around my daughter and cocooned her in a faint, esoteric mist as tendrils of the Necroverse's infinite sorrow slithered into orifices, sank beneath the epidermis, sought out the very core of my daughter and somehow reported back to these two women. One just turned forty-seven today, the other many, many years older. Peth was ancient, but had a flawless, pale complexion, frustratingly beautiful hair, and commanded respect. She drove me fucking nuts.

That's what you get for kidnapping a demented witch's daughter then marrying her the next day. Some people simply won't ever forgive such minor transgressions!

After ten nervous minutes, the inspection was over and it was clear the healing had already begun. They withdrew gradually from their whispers, both drained, Peth particularly so after her morph. I could only imagine how exhausted she was.

"She's going to be fine," said Phage with relief. "No internal injuries. Just the arm and leg. Broken bones."

"What about her chest? She's got tire marks all over her."

"Just bruising, nothing more," noted Peth.

"So no ambulance?" I asked.

"Best not to if we don't need it." Phage rubbed at her face; she just wanted what was best for Jen.

"If you're positive?"

"Yes. You saw what she did out there. We can't risk that happening in the hospital when she wakes up. We whispered for her to sleep. Her mind is at rest. We can repair her, but she'll still need a cast and looking after. What are we going to do, Soph?"

"You have your note, I assume?" asked Peth, matter-of-fact. "Oh, and happy birthday, my dear. I can stay with Jen and Soph while you do what must be done. Jen will be in safe hands."

Phage and I exchanged worried glances. I nodded.

"Actually, the note is for both of us," Phage told her mother. "Our names are on it. We both have to leave."

"Interesting," said Peth, frowning a little, then clearly thinking, a faraway look in her eyes. After a moment, she snapped back to the present and said, "Has anything happened? Why this? Why now? It's you, isn't it?" She glowered at me. Damn, she was one hostile old bint.

"Lots has happened," I told her. "Not much I can tell you. But yeah, something is going on. I've been shown things. I was told things. Jen is special, and it's tied up with that. But it seems I've been singled-out, shown glimpses I don't think anyone else knows. Not that I'm going to do anything with the information. There's nothing I can do, but still." I left it at that, unsure if I'd already said more than was allowed.

"I assumed as much. We have been watching you, Soph. I have been watching you, as is my right. You are of age now, and well known. You are being tested. I presume we're talking about glimpses of the Necroverse?" I nodded.

"And your yearly notes, those you kill, they tell you things? They wish to stop you? See what your family, and my family, I must stress, may become?"

"Yeah, something like that."

"Jen is a special girl. She has gifts I have never encountered in one so young. She has the knowledge of the sisters buried deep. A rarity in our world. There are those who would stop such a blessing. It clouds the future. So you are being tested. You are seeing behind the veil. Glimpses. But you will never know the truth."

"I don't want to bloody know," I shouted. "I want to be left alone. I want my little girl to be safe."

"Then you must both go. Fulfill the note. It is not unheard of. There must be a reason for such an undertaking. I will stay with Jen. She will be protected."

"What is this leading up to, Mother? Why has Soph been shown things? I wish you could tell me," she said, the tears falling as the stress hit her now the adrenaline was dissipating.

"I've told you what I could. What Mawr told me. About there being something in our future. My future. About Jen being special. And the eyes, with the notes. I told you what I could, what wasn't part of the note. I'm not even sure I should talk about any of it. I don't know the bloody rules. They never tell you. Ugh, fucking nightmare. Lakes of goddamn lava sucking up dead shifters, notes being written, ominous foretelling of the future. It's like some sick joke nobody will tell me the punchline to."

"You saw the notes being created?" Peth's eyes tried to bore into my soul. "You saw a body taken by the Necroverse? And you know Mawr? Where is he? What is he to you?"

"Now's not the time for any of this, okay? We're babbling away when Jen is hurt. Can you fix her or not?" I held Peth's gaze. She was scary, and way more powerful than I'd ever be, but she knew I would never bow to her, could never back down, and that was why our relationship was, shall we say, strained?

"As you wish. But we must talk, and today. First, food and caffeine. Lots of caffeine. I am exhausted after the trip, and we have much work ahead of us. Tomorrow you may leave, but today, and tonight, there is healing to be performed."

I grunted at Peth and Phage, then went to rifle through the kitchen and the shopping still not put away. Phage put an arm to my shoulder and said, "I'll cook. You only got home yesterday. You need to rest too."

"I'll rest when I know my daughter is safe. When I know she will be alright."

"She will, Soph. You trust me, don't you?"

"Of course."

"Then don't worry. Mother and I will heal our daughter."

"What has been going on here!" demanded Peth, as Woofer materialized in front of us all then licked Jen's hand.

"Jen is hurt?" asked Woofer, ears flat to his head, tail between his legs.

"She'll be okay, buddy. Still morphing then, I see?"

"Woofer was locked outside. Heard shouting. Couldn't get in. So thought about Jen and came."

"I think there is much to discuss. Daughter of mine, did you not think to tell me that your pet, a creature not of the Necroverse, has gained such strong abilities?"

"In case you didn't know, Mother, which you did, Soph has been in the hospital. He nearly died, and you were nowhere to be seen. If you want to know things, keep in touch with us. Otherwise, we're fine without you."

"I come when needed. Why is this dog staring at me?"

"Play ball with Woofer?" the poor guy asked, staring up at Peth with hope in his eyes while his tail swished back and forth across the death rug.

"No, I will not. Shoo. We have work to do."

"What did he say?" asked Phage.

"He asked your mother why she's such a bitch," I thought. Out loud, I said, "Woofer's just relieved Jen is alive and wanted to play fetch with Peth."

"Oh. Maybe Soph will play with you later, Woofer," Phage told him. "But now we must eat lots of food so Mother and I can fix Jen. You be a good boy, okay?"

Woofer moved over to Phage for an ear rub then looked at me. I nodded, and he curled up beside Jen and remained there, refusing to move, even with Peth glaring at him. It was the proudest I'd ever been of my dopey dog. If he could endure that, he was truly part of the family. Our family. Phage, Jen, and me. And unfortunately, Pethach.

It was going to be a long night.

After eating a hearty meal in the living room while we kept a worried eye on Jen, and several pots of disgusting coffee that got worse every week—a new brand that promised the taste of Brazil, but was more like the taste of a Brazilian's crotch and was presumably made with their shaved pubic hair ground to dust then flavored with sweat squeezed from skimpy underwear—Phage and her mother got down to some serious whispering.

I wasn't allowed to remain in the room. Peth had a real thing about anyone, especially men, and super-especially me, overhearing her whispers. I got it. It was secret, the result of centuries of strict training, and it could cause irrevocable harm to those not of the sisterhood. But I still took it personally.

"What should I do about the hit-and-run driver? I got the registration," I asked Phage as I came back into the room while they were on a break.

"Kill the coward," said Peth without looking up from inspecting Jen's recovering wounds. The bone was back in place, now the knitting together was next.

"Phage?"

She turned from our daughter, looked into my eyes, and said, "Yes, kill him. He drove off after believing he killed our little girl. He doesn't deserve to live."

I nodded to her. I left to go kill the guy.

Then I ambled back in. "Oops. Forgot the registration." I left.

And then I returned once more. "Um, anyone know how to trace a car registration? I haven't got a clue." Both women stared at me, incredulous. "What?" I held my hands out, questioning. "How would I know?"

"You're a Necro known all over the country for your prowess, and your reputation precedes you everywhere you go." Peth glared at me.

"Does not. Um, does it?"

"Yes!" they both replied.

"That's not good."

"So how have you managed all these years without being able to trace a registration?" asked Peth.

"I'm not a bloody detective. It isn't like on the TV where you can just call someone up and they'll give you the information."

Peth phoned someone up and they gave her the information.

Bitch.

I wrote it down, and then I left. Again. And I only came back once more.

"What now?" they shouted.

I think they might have been a bit fed up with my dithering. To be fair, I was worried beyond belief, still weak as a kitten, and had expected a quiet day with my family. I'd forgotten it was Phage's birthday, I had a Necronote to fulfill, and I wanted more sexy times. All I got was a half-dead daughter and my mother-in-law.

"Hey, no need to be like that. It's a present, for you," I told Phage. "It should probably wait, but, er, well, it might be important. Might be able to help. Mawr said she could."

"And we need to talk about Mawr," said Peth. "That horrible old man and his snooping. Where is he?"

"None of your business. He helped me out a lot when I was a kid. He's a nice guy. He gave me something I didn't want, but he insisted. She didn't help when I needed her, and I don't like the idea of having her, anyway. But Phage, I know you adore this kind of stuff. So, here." I reached for the oversized matchbox on the mantelpiece, then offered it to Phage with a sheepish smile.

"Ooh, matches." She smiled, eyes twinkling. I think every muscle in my body relaxed. If she had her twinkle back, Jen was really going to be fine.

"God, I can't believe I'm doing this with Jen lying there like this. Is she truly okay?"

"Yes, she honestly is." Phage rose and we hugged tight. "She's sleeping, her bones are back in place, and tomorrow when she wakes up she'll be hurting like hell, have a cast on her leg, but be fine. Just rather disorientated, and maybe forgetful. Honestly, she will make a fast and full recovery. Mother is the best at this," she whispered.

"Okay, if you're sure?"

"Yes. Now, what's with the box?"

"Take it. Mawr said the box is indestructible and he's right. I battered it some, but she didn't help me. And I know you and the fae."

"Fae?" Phage's eyebrows rose.

"Yeah, you love them, right? Always saying you wanted to see one. Well, now's your chance. But don't be disappointed," I added, squirming under Peth's icy glare.

The women gathered around and I handed the matchbox to Phage.

"It can't be a faery," said Peth. "Nobody's seen them since the Queen went missing about a thousand years ago."

"Don't ask me. He just said her name was Malka and —"

"That's impossible!" Peth gasped.

"Haha, you're such a kidder." Phage looked at me, questioning. I shrugged.

"What?"

"This can't be Malka," insisted Peth.

"Who's Malka?"

"The Queen!" they both shouted.

"What? The *Queen* queen. The faery Queen? Never heard of her."

"That's because you aren't a witch, or a wizard. Just a big brute with way too much luck," hissed Peth.

"Ah, now we're getting to it. That's what you think of me, isn't it?"

"Yes." Peth glared, I glared, Phage slapped us both across the cheek.

"What was that for?" I asked.

"For shouting. And because I love you." She grinned, then kissed me in front of her mother. She slid the lid aside and we peered in at the tiny dormouse. A beautiful scent, like a cuddle to the nostrils, made me shiver.

"Malka," whispered Peth.

"Look at her little nose twitching. She's so cute," said Phage, smiling.

"She is a cutie, isn't she? Mawr said she would come when I called if I really needed her, but she didn't. I was almost dead, utterly desperate, but I summoned her and I guess she decided I wasn't worth the trouble. I know nothing about fae, figured you'd want her. Do you?"

"Oh, yes. Of course. Are you sure? It's Malka. *The* Malka."

"Missing for a thousand years. Longer," agreed Peth. "The missing Queen. Key to the realms of faery."

"See, this is exactly why I gave her to you. I don't want to get mixed up in that. It sounds awful. All the stories I've heard about fae, well, they sound like trouble. All sparkly stuff and messing with everything. No thank you very much. But I know you witches have a thing about them. What gives?"

They looked at me, aghast, like I was missing an ear.

"You really don't know?" asked Phage. "Soph, this is an amazing gift. It's beyond priceless. It's incredible. It's Malka. The first faery. Queen of all fae."

"Yeah, so you keep saying. So? She won't even wake up. And what if Malka does? What will you do with her? I've got enough to worry about. I shouldn't have given her to you. Here, I'll stick the Queen in the attic. We can forget all about her."

"No." Phage snatched Malka close to her chest. The dormouse snuffled, then put her tiny paws over her face and curled up tight into a ball. She began to snore.

"Incredible." Peth couldn't take her eyes off the mouse.

"Well, anyway. I have something to do. Damn, I'm knackered. But I'm gonna kill that bastard. Bye. See you later."

I don't think either one of them noticed I'd gone. See, this was exactly what I was worried about. Our daughter's life was in peril, I was off to kill the man who hurt her, and all they could do was stare at a matchbox with a bloody dormouse inside.

It's why I have always hated magic. And always will. It takes people away from what is truly important. Biscuits, family, and sleeping.

Would You?

Killing somebody because it's you or them is hard enough. Beyond hard. Most people couldn't do it. It is terrifying. It is visceral. Your heart feels like it's ready to explode, you are scared beyond belief, panicked, and you have to actually do the deed. Not push a button and *bam*, they're dead, but get up close and see the blood pumping, feel their brains warm on your hand, watch the life fade from their eyes.

It is beyond most people, even when confronted with their own death.

I am capable of such things. I can kill in such a way even when not in the throes of true bloodlust, where I think nothing, feel nothing, merely go berserker and destroy them without there being any doubt of my victory. It terrifies them. My conviction is flawless, my confidence utter, and no matter the wounds I receive, I carry on as I don't even notice them because I am lost to the fight. To the horror and the strange beauty of being a master of my own destiny for that one brief moment when it is them or me.

But when you're worried sick about your child? When she is lying in a recliner in your living room but should be in the hospital? Yeah, that's different.

As I cycled or pushed my bike through the frosty streets of Shrewsbury, the rooftops still covered in a light dusting of snow, but the roads clear, I had plenty of time to think about what I was preparing to do, and the fucked-up position my family was currently in. Why had I let Jen be tended to at home? She had broken bones, nearly died, and I'd just spent months in the hospital because of severe internal complications and repeated bouts of sepsis.

Because I trusted my wife. And god help me, when it came to Jen, I even trusted Peth. If they said she'd be fine, then I believed them. If they said it was merely broken bones and their whispers could fix them, then yes, I believed them. It did not sit well, but it sat better than it would if I was still Phage's age. For I recalled a time when there were no hospitals, when nobody knew the importance of washing your hands before sticking them into somebody's body.

If you broke a bone back then you were screwed. Deformed for life. If it was something internal, then you died. Plain and simple. Phage had never experienced that world. She lived in a time when the NHS accepted all, and doctors, nurses, and surgeons did everything they could to save you, no matter your background. And it was free. What a world.

So if Phage grew up with the wonders of modern medicine and took it for granted, yet said Jen could stay home, then I accepted it.

Didn't stop me worrying like hell as I trudged up a steep, icy hill on the outskirts of town, the streets dark. No lights, no cars, no buses, no nothing. I was alone here. The world was turned off for another day in the hopes it would still be there tomorrow.

I paused at the top of the hill and checked the route on my phone. Such a simple act switched me into Necronote mode. This was how I worked. I got a location; I went and killed somebody. This time, I even had a reason beyond saving my own skin.

It was to save somebody else's. If this dude did this once, he could do it again. Him, or a child? It was no choice at all. And yet I had an issue with it. This wasn't kill or be killed. No fight to the death I couldn't avoid. I was walking into this of my own free will. I could call the police. They would see Jen, they could trace the guy, and he'd be held accountable. But Jen was already halfway healed, meaning the driver would get a slap on the wrist, a short spell in prison maybe. That wasn't enough. That was nowhere near enough.

I sailed alongside the river Severn on a bike path through the park, then took several turns until I was past the city and into the countryside once more. Only the almost full moon lit my way. I turned off my bike light, and rode carefully along a lane then took a turn down a rough track to the owner's registered address. Easing to a stop, I pushed my bike into the trees and stepped back to ensure it was hidden. My legs were on fire; the exercise had taken its toll after so little for so long.

With nothing but my trusty knife and my phone, I was traveling light, which was good, so I kept to the tree line and crept towards a smart cottage with a gravel drive and an expensive oak gate. I heard banging about from a detached garage and saw the tail end of the car sticking out. He was in there, maybe beating out the dent? I didn't care.

Before I confronted him, I hopped the low wall and dashed across the garden then peered in through windows. The kitchen was a mess. Pots, pans, plates, and crap everywhere. No sign of kids. I checked through the living room window. A single lamp cast dull light. The TV was on. Junk spilled everywhere. On the edge of the ratty sofa were piles of blankets and a sleeping bag. A fire burned low in a rusting, ancient stove. He was alone. No family. No need to worry about freaking out children, or me having second thoughts.

I walked back over to the garage, stealth unnecessary now as I wasn't gonna kill him before having a chat first. He was still banging away in there, and swearing. The lights were on, so he either had a private source or was careful most of the time with his quota.

The garage was large enough for two cars, but he only had the one, and before I got close I could smell the stink of bootleg petrol and bootleg booze in equal amounts. As I crunched up to the back of the Subaru, I confirmed the plate. This was my guy. The garage was stacked high with shelving full of demijohns of homemade wine, beer, and who knew what else. There were dozens of petrol canisters of all shapes and sizes, so this guy clearly did more than his fair share of driving. The place reeked, and I didn't even want to think how volatile it was. One match and *poof*.

A tool thudded onto the painted concrete floor. He grunted, then came around from the front and stopped dead when he saw me standing at the doorway.

"Hello," I snarled.

"Who the fuck are you?" He swigged from a glass tumbler, then downed it.

"I'm the father of the girl you just ran over." I flipped the popper on the leather strip that held my knife tight into its sheath. His eyes followed my slow movement and he screamed, "Get away from me!" Spittle flew from his mouth. "It was an accident. She was in the road. I couldn't stop. I skidded."

"You were driving like a fucking moron. Way too fast. And pissed, by the looks of it. You think it's okay to drive around the lanes off your skull? It had been bloody snowing."

"I had a hard day," he mumbled. "All this shit. No fucking power, no fucking food. Nothing but this gutrot and this goddamn crappy petrol. It's fucked up my car. The engine's knackered, I think. It was an accident. I didn't mean it."

"You didn't stop," I said, a calm taking me over. The calm before the storm.

"And what? You gonna kill me? Haha. Go on, call the police, see if I care. I've got nothing left to lose. The wife left, took the kids, and I've got a shitty job stuck at my bloody computer all day with hardly enough to eat, nowhere to go, nothing to do. I just wanted to blow off some steam," he pleaded, eyes filling with tears. "I just needed to do something. Get out, you know?"

"I know, sure. But you hit my baby girl and you were drunk. You didn't stop."

"Fuck off. Go on, get lost. I don't need this crap from you. You aren't going to kill me. People don't do that. Look at you, with your fucking hair and your bloody muscles. You're a pathetic, vain arsehole. All looks and no substance. I know your sort." He was getting braver, carried away by the booze and the fact he thought, for some strange reason, I was a preening dickhead, instead of a violent arsehole. "Yeah, that's what I thought. Bet you've never even been in a fight in your whole life, have you?"

I was so pissed off with this idiot that I wanted to scare him, freak him out. I held his gaze as I stripped off my jacket then my shirt, partly because I wanted him fearful, partly because I didn't want to ruin another shirt. They were hard to come by now, and I knew I'd never find another the same.

"You think this is all for show?" I asked as I folded up my shirt, placed it on a shelf, and turned three-sixty.

His eyes went wide as he took in my ruined body, the latest scar at my side still red and angry after months.

"I... I'm sorry. Okay, let's talk. I can pay. Not much. Here, take the car. It's yours."

"You just said it was knackered."

"What do you want then?" There was real terror in his eyes now. He backed up to the rear wall and grabbed a stubby length of pipe. He hefted it, slapped it into his palm, and his confidence returned. But it was the confidence of a foolish drunken man who was only half-aware of what the deal was here.

I walked forward, drew my knife, and told him, "I'm going to kill you. Not for hurting my daughter, but because you were drunk and you didn't stop. Do you understand?"

He wet himself, and the fight went from his eyes. I stepped up and he swung hard at my head, as that's what you would do. He wasn't a fighter, knew nothing, and I simply ducked. As the bar continued its arc, I closed the gap and, with our eyes locked, I stabbed him right in the heart. He sucked in a deep breath, his face contorted in pain and shock, then the bar clattered to the ground as he slumped down, bleeding out.

I found a lighter amongst all the crap and set fire to the garage after pouring out the fuel. I walked away, not bothering to look back, as what was the point?

Feeling dejected about the state of the world, I got my bike from the bushes and rode away.

I wondered what he meant about my hair. I thought it was nice.

A Dark Night

When I arrived home, I was freezing, weary, bitter, twisted, and questioning my actions. After stowing my bike, I stood outside the front door as the snow fell gently, the world silent and still, and I couldn't go in.

Why had I done that? What gave me the right? This was no magical voodoo. Not a crime I had to commit. There were options. Who was I to decide who lived and who died? A downtrodden guy with no hope, no future, no wife or kids, no loving family, had gone off the deep end because he was miserable and might well have been suffering from depression.

Shouldn't he have been offered help rather than death? What kind of a monster did that make me? I was conflicted, just as I had been my entire life. He nearly killed my daughter, and he would have undoubtedly got behind the wheel drunk again, but what if he'd been arrested? Maybe he would have turned his life around. Maybe.

I was truthful enough with myself to understand that part of me wanted to do it. Not for revenge, not to safeguard the future of others, to take this menace off the roads once and for all, but because I'd had no excitement, no adrenaline rush for months, and I missed it.

The buzz.

The fear.

The hunt.

God help me, I missed it. Had that been it? This murder was nothing but a damaged soldier craving the thrill of battle. To feel alive after being half-dead for months.

Sometimes I scared myself.

Finally, I let myself in, removed my boots, and tiptoed into the living room. Jen was asleep with a cast on her leg. Phage was squeezed onto the recliner beside her, dead to the world. Woofer was on the murder rug, curled up and snoring. Peth was standing by the stove, lost deep in thought. The orange glow of the fire bounced off her white clothes, sending dancing shadows into the corners of our living room.

She turned, and scrutinized me. Damn, she was cold. I mimed the universal action for a cuppa and she nodded back, so I headed to the kitchen and put the kettle on.

I made the tea and slumped into a chair. This had been a long day; I was exhausted. Was it always like this at home? Were there always things going on? Crap happening? I liked to think ours was a peaceful, happy home for the most part, but it was anything but. There was always some nonsense or other that cropped up, and today had been no exception. Dwarves in my chair this morning, notes when I'd believed I had the better part of a year to put my feet up, and now my daughter getting hurt and my freaky mother-in-law apparently here to stay and run the fort while my wife and I went on a joint murder spree. You couldn't make this shit up. Not that I'd want to.

"How is she?" I asked, as Peth glided into the room and took a seat.

She took a moment to sip her tea. Her face was drawn, with dark rings under her eyes. The whispers took it out of the witches, even one as experienced as Peth. And the morph she'd accomplished was no mean feat. Bet she despised that I did it better!

After another sip, keeping me waiting, the bitch, she set her tea down and said, "Jen will be absolutely fine. Her arm is mended completely. It may be rather stiff, but that's all. Her tibia was snapped clean in half, but it's already knotting back together. She'll need the cast for a while, but my guess is that in a week or two it will be like it never happened."

"Great, that's great. Thanks for your help. We appreciate it."

Peth nodded. "You know she is a remarkable child, don't you? That she isn't the same as other Necros her age. Not like many twice her age."

"I know. It's a worry."

"You should feel blessed. Jen will be a powerful witch, and so much more. A dragon of her own. A unicorn. With her gifts, her as-yet-unknown abilities, she will be a force to be reckoned with in the magical community."

"That's her choice, but let's get one thing straight, Peth. I don't want her to be part of the so-called magical community. Poking her nose into business that doesn't concern her or anyone else. Dabbling in this shit you call magic. I don't want that life for her. You witches are all the same. You see it as a gift, a blessing, when the whole fucking thing is a curse. It's bad enough we risk our lives once a year, you lot go out of your way to do it on a daily basis. I do not want to lose my little girl."

Peth held back her anger and said, "As you say, it is not your choice. She says things she cannot know, sees things she shouldn't be able to see. And Phage tells me that Jen healed herself momentarily after her accident? That is not something we should take lightly. I have never heard of such a thing. It requires investigation."

"It's because of your bloody training," I whispered, not wanting to wake anyone. "I know you've started teaching Jen some of what you know. You're showing her things she's too young to understand."

"I have done no such thing. I know you think I am corrupting her, but I promise you, and trust me, I have no need for your approval or trust, that I have done nothing in terms of teaching. At most, I've answered a few questions, nothing more. I am merely watching. As you say, she is too young. Her brain is still forming. I would not interfere before the time is right. She is my granddaughter. I wish her no harm."

"And she's my daughter. Never forget that, Peth. She is my daughter."

"And I acknowledge that. I will guide her when the time is right, when we all agree. She needs me. She will need my knowledge, and if she wishes, I will train her in the ways of my sisters. Witches follow many paths, hers is yet to be decided."

"Thank you. And sorry, I'm just stressed. People want to stop her already, Peth. I can't speak of it, it was part of my note, but there are Necros out there who see her future and want to end it. What do you think about Phage's note?"

"It is bad timing."

"And?"

"Most unusual, but not unheard of. The notes endure."

"Yeah, yeah." I waved her crap away. "But this is different. I'm telling you, I'm being shown things. I don't know if it's on purpose, or something inside me is able to see this stuff, but either way, it's not helping me sleep at night."

"Soph, much as I hate to say this, you are a unique man. You have abilities you don't even begin to understand, maybe even know about. You are determined, you have survived longer than most and had harder jobs than any other Necro male, as far as I'm aware. Your gifts are more limited than many, but you are known. Others know your name, your strengths, and your weaknesses. Don't let them deceive you, or make you fail, by playing on those weaknesses. I too have seen the possible futures for you all, but I will tell you one thing. Nothing, absolutely nothing, is certain in this world."

"Not even taxes?" I joked.

"Not even taxes." Peth didn't even crack a smile.

"I keep hearing this about myself. That other Necros know of me, that I'm different. But I'm not. I just do what I have to. That's it."

"Yes, but you keep on doing it. Year after year. You survive. You change. You adapt. You learn fast, and you abide by the rules. How many others are there of your age? Men, I mean."

"There's my neighbor. And Mawr, and well, I've heard there are others. I've met some, but I killed them."

"There are a handful, that's about it. Only the best survive. All of us are given insights as we get older. I have seen things too. It is our lot. Our burden or our reward. You choose what it is to be. But do not push too hard. Never read too much into it. This is the way. This is the path. Don't try to understand too much or you will perish."

"I don't want to see any of it. But I keep being given glimpses, told things. Hints, half-truths. Like it's leading somewhere. Is it?"

"No. As I said, once you reach a certain level, you are allowed to know more. Or your innate abilities allow you to see. It is merely the way of things, nothing more. It means nothing. It is simply to allow you to continue. To make it to the next year."

"But why? What's the fucking point of it all?"

"Why are we here at all? Why does the universe exist? How is it possible for a planet to coalesce from stardust then transform into an environment capable of supporting life? How is it that from tiny, mindless creatures we evolved into human beings, and that for the entire history of our world, every one of your ancestors managed to survive and pass on their DNA? That's a much bigger question."

She paused to take another sip of her tea. We listened to the soft breathing from the other room before she continued.

"Soph, there are billions of stars in our galaxy, trillions of galaxies. Do you honestly believe that this means anything at all? These things we do? These trifling questions we have? Even the notes themselves? It's nothing. It is no great mystery. It pales in comparison to the majesty and utter strangeness of the universe. It's utterly unimportant. We are but stardust. Why concern yourself with the notes and their provenance? It is merely the way of things. Is it so strange? I think not. Some questions can never be answered. Some things simply are."

"Way to put a downer on a guy's first day out of the hospital."

"We do what we can to protect our own. We live our lives as we see fit. But I will offer you this advice, Necrosoph. Do not ever apologize for the things you do. Because, and I promise you this, nobody cares and it is all utterly meaningless. In a million years, do you think your actions will be remembered? That it will have made a difference? No. Humans pass the time in any way they can to stop themselves going utterly insane. That's all we're doing. Passing time until we die. And then the real fun begins." Peth held my gaze, and she smiled. She actually smiled.

"Tell me another time? But thanks. I think." I grinned. Somehow, her words were a comfort. Finding the whole situation bizarre, I did what any self-respecting Englishman would do and I made more tea. We'd never spoken for so long, and I knew this conversation wasn't over. Peth was biding her time, getting me in the right frame of mind so she could ask her questions. I figured that, for once, I'd actually answer them.

I placed the tea down then said, "Go on then, ask."

"Oh, I assume you killed the man." Peth waved it away as unimportant.

"I did. But not that. I know you want to."

"Very well." Peth pouted; she hated being second-guessed. "Where is Mawr? How do you know him? And how did he have Malka?"

"I met him when I was young. After a few notes. He guided me, calmed me down, showed me how to control my anger, release it when needed. He taught me many things. I stayed with him, then I left."

"He was a good man. But he has been missing for many years."

"Yeah, he likes it that way."

"And where is he?"

"I can't tell you. If he wants you to know, he'll tell you. Why is it so important?"

"He is a very knowledgeable man." Peth sighed, but there was something going on here. I honestly didn't have the energy to care.

"Suit yourself. And what about the mouse? Why is she so important?"

"She is the Queen! There is no more important creature. Missing for millennia. Now Mawr gives her to you. What is that old man up to?"

"He said she would help me. She didn't. I figured Phage would want her. She likes your witch mystery, magic stuff."

"Why must you dismiss it so? You could do wondrous things if you were so minded." Peth leaned forward, rested her chin on her fist, and studied me.

"I am not so minded. I don't like it. I don't want to cast spells and look under magical rocks. I want to rest easy and not have my mind corrupted. I don't want to whisper. I don't want to see the future. I want my family to be safe. That's it."

"You are a strange fellow, but I admire your conviction. Soph, the wonders I have seen. The things you could know. But as you say, it is your choice. Malka is important, so if he gave her to you, there must have been good reason. How did he come to have her, I wonder?"

I shrugged. "Beats me. He's always up to all sorts. Maybe the sneaky bugger meant for me to give her to Phage. I wouldn't put it past him. You lot do like to work in mysterious ways, don't you? Why say something straight when you can convolute it and put a magical edge on it?"

"Haha, we do like to play our little games. It keeps us amused through the ages. Now we must decide what to do with Malka."

"Let her sleep. I'm sure she'll wake up when it's the most inconvenient. What would you do with her? Get a faery army and kill all wizards, is that the idea?"

"No, of course not! But she is the key to their land. Fae are locked there, and there is no entry from this side. With Malka, the way could be opened."

"And we'd have a horde of impossibly beautiful, sickly sweet fae running amok? Ta, but no thank you. Leave her be. Oh, while we're on the subject of weird, wibbly wobbly magic, what's with Woofer? Any ideas?"

"I have one. And I suspect it is correct. Let it wait until the morning. I have the distinct impression that Woofer and Jen have been doing things they shouldn't. We need a word with your dragon too. Sleep well. And Soph?"

"Yes?"

Peth rose and moved to the kitchen door. "Look after my daughter. She is capable, more capable than any of my other children, and I love her dearly. Do not let her die."

"I won't."

Peth was gone.

I probably had a lot to think about but my mind was empty. I practically crawled up the stairs and was asleep the moment I slid under the covers.

"Welcome home, Soph," I mumbled, as I sank gratefully into oblivion.

So Gross

"Come on then," I said, "what have you and Woofer been up to?"

Jen blushed and stared at the cast on her leg, which was propped up on a dining chair. "What do you mean?"

"I mean, Woofer keeps morphing, and he most definitely isn't supposed to be able to. He's being a very naughty boy."

"Woofer good dog." His ears flattened.

"You are a good dog, mostly. But good dogs don't appear on the roof. They most definitely don't appear in the fridge. You could have died if I hadn't gone for milk." I'd found him there this morning; god knows how he fit.

"Woofer likes sausages."

"Yes, I know you do. Now let me talk to Jen."

Phage turned from the kitchen counter and took a chair opposite Jen. Peth sat, staring at Jen with eyes that should make any granddaughter spill the beans instantly. She was itching to know the answers, although she most definitely already knew.

"You can tell them, you know," Peth encouraged. "I think I know, and it's certainly a strange thing to do, but we must be sure."

"Do I have to?" Jen was almost crimson.

"Honey, we worry about you. You got run over, you fixed your broken bones, then got up and wandered off. But you collapsed. You can't be doing things like that. You could have made it worse."

"But I feel fine," she protested. "And I promise I won't do it again. I hope that driver gets thrown in jail."

Phage and I exchanged a glance. We'd already spoken about the guy, so Phage knew what I'd done. She'd also held me as I cried. Told me it was alright. I knew it wasn't. It was wrong.

"What did you do?" asked Phage.

"I... We... It's going to sound so silly."

"Just tell us."

"When you were in the hospital, I... er... well... Woofer started to morph. You know that bit. He kept appearing in weird places. I asked him about it, but he didn't know why he could do it. So I... I... well, I decided to follow him. He... Okay, here it is. He ate Tyr's poo, okay? I looked it up, and, er, well, it seems like dragon poo can, you know, let you do stuff. It's a thing. People do it if they're lucky enough to have a dragon. Which nobody else is."

"Dragon poo? Woofer, have you been eating Tyr's poo?"

"Woofer likes it. Taste of chicken. We eat now?"

"It so does not taste of chicken! It's utterly gross, and I only did it once. Okay, maybe twice. Okay three, but the last time I swallowed it with lots of water so it wasn't so bad. That was yesterday morning, before school. I felt weird all day and did some cool stuff, but that's all."

"Let me get this straight. You're telling me that you and Woofer have been eating shit and it gives you powers? Is that what I'm hearing?"

Jen was purple now, squirming like a fish on a hook. "Yes. Sorry. Ugh, I know it sounds so nasty, and I feel sick just thinking about it, but I just wanted to try a bit."

"This is..." Phage shook her head, then she smiled. I caught her eye and I couldn't help myself. I burst out laughing. Phage soon followed, then Jen laughed too, more from relief than anything.

"I'm sorry. I know it's stupid and disgusting, but it works! It really does."

"How'd you find out about this?" I asked. "And Peth, you knew, didn't you?"

"I had my suspicions after what you told me yesterday. And with Woofer morphing like that. I knew something was happening."

"Why would Tyr's droppings do this?" I mused.

Peth's eyes bored into my skull. I think she was trying to set my brain on fire. "Because he's a dragon. Every ounce of him is pure magic. He's everything the Necroverse strives to be. He's immortal, cannot be harmed, needs blood, and preferably Necro blood to grow, and his pellets may be the waste product of his needs, but they still contain valuable matter. It's part of him. Contains his essence."

"How the hell do you know that?"

"Because I do. I read. I study. I learn things. Try to understand."

She was having a dig at me, but I couldn't be arsed to argue. There were more important things to worry about. Like my daughter eating shit off the ground.

"Jen, how did you learn about it? I mean, what, you just followed Woofer then copied him? Why did you think it would do anything?"

"Dad, there's this thing called the internet you know. I had a hunch so I looked it up."

"Don't get smart," I laughed. "What, there's info about dragon poo on the web? Come on? Who would put that there?"

"Not the regular web, no. I, er, did some digging recently. You and Mum are always going on about Necro this and Necro that. I wanted to learn more."

Oh, bugger, here we go, I thought. Kids grow up too fast these days. I knew I was right to blame the internet. "So where did you look? And yes, I know we still need to have a chat about things. But it seems like you already know more than we thought."

"I looked up Necro stuff, and I came across the Necronet. It's like the dark web but, well, it's for Necros."

"Jen!" scolded Phage. "You'll be traced. People will be watching. You should never do things like that. Now they'll know."

"Who will? What are you talking about? It's just the internet. It's not a super-secret conspiracy. Is it?" Jen looked at each of us in turn. She was worried when she saw our faces.

"Honey, that's exactly what it is. A secret never to be told to anyone. The Necroverse is a very dangerous place. The most dangerous place."

"What is the Necroverse?"

"Everything," I told her, waving my hand. "The world. More specifically, the world we inhabit. One filled with dragons and unicorns and mad witches. A dangerous place. If you search online for things to do with it, you will be monitored, we can guarantee it. So be careful. And for god's sake don't talk to anyone, and I mean anyone, about it apart from family. Okay?"

"Okay. You're making me worried now. Did I do the wrong thing?"

"No, it's fine," said Phage, smiling to calm her down. "But Dad's right. You must be careful. I think you better show us what you've been looking at."

It was a different world. Jen clicked expertly around the laptop, going deeper and deeper into the inner world of the web. How she navigated this stuff I couldn't fathom. There were endless passwords to be input, redirects and dead ends, strange pages that baffled me, and then she was into what looked like the regular internet but was far from it.

"Fucking hell," I blurted. "It's got everything here. Fuck!"

"Dad! I thought we agreed, no swearing."

"Sorry, but shit, look at it all. How much have you read?"

"Not much. I was looking for info about dragons. I got involved in that, but I read a few other pages. Is it true?"

"Is what true?" My heart sank. She wasn't ready for the truth. I couldn't handle the truth.

"That Necros live forever? Or that some can? People with gifts like ours, although, um, I still don't know what yours and Mum's are apart from you talking to the animals. Are you going to tell me today?"

"No, not today. But soon, I promise. And to answer your question, yes, some people with special gifts can live very long lives. But nobody lives forever, and you can die just as easily as anyone else. We aren't like Tyr, or Mr. Wonderful, or even Bernard. We die easily."

"Gosh. Wow! This is for real? You aren't joking? I figured maybe this Necronet was a bit of a joke. You know, like a role playing thing. Like a wiki for a game or something. It's real? Will I live forever?" Her eyes were like saucers; we were screwed. No way would she stay away from this.

"It's real," said Phage. "But you are too young to learn much. You shouldn't be reading any of this yet. Come on, it's time to get you sorted out. No school today. Not with that leg and the night you had. I already called. You can hang out at home, but come Monday it's back to school. Okay?"

"Awesome!"

Phage gave me a look, then helped Jen up the stairs to get ready for the day. Peth glared at me like it was all my fault, then left too, and I was finally alone in the kitchen with my dumb dog and the laptop.

"Fucking internet. I knew it was your fault," I hissed at the laptop, like it could hear me. Maybe it could, or at least somebody somewhere was probably listening, watching. Our lives recorded to be mulled over to see if we needed to be eliminated for transgressions real or otherwise.

Damn, I missed the old days. Give me a quill and parchment any day.

And yet, I couldn't help but wonder.

With a sneaky glance to check nobody was watching, I had a peek at the Necronet. It was fucking awesome!

Think Wikipedia but for Necros. There was page after page of it. Endless. From first inspection, a lot of it was drivel. Nutty ancient witches and wizards gagging at the thought of finally sharing their knowledge with the world. Except, most was anything but knowledge. Just the rantings and ravings of deluded old folk who should know better.

There was, however, a surprising amount of top-notch information. No secrets, nary a mention of the Necronotes, thank goodness. Although, I was sure I'd find it eventually, same as Jen could. What there was though, were numerous entries concerning the many and varied skills Necros had. There were detailed studies on how to progress with your gifts, information about zoolingualism—a very common Necro trait—and a fair few entries on morphing in its many variations. From my style of travel, to the animorph, or shifter, it had it all. I certainly didn't have the time, or inclination, to read it all, and it was clear much was merely conjecture, but I could see that it would suck Jen into the world.

I hunted around furtively for the information on dragons and found an entire world within a world. Necros sure did love their dragons. It was a reminder to redouble our efforts to keep Tyr hidden. Necros would do just about anything to get their hands on one, not just because of their power, but because of the strength and gifts they could give to other Necros. It wasn't something I'd really considered, how prized they were for the magic they possessed, but it was obvious it would be tempting.

And there it was, all about dragon scat. Jen was right! The poo was relatively rare, as the older the dragon became, the less they defecated as they became increasingly efficient at metabolizing everything they consumed. I already knew they never urinated—Tyr had never drunk anything but blood in his whole life—but hadn't known about the poo side of things. After all, who dwells on poo unless you're the proud parent of a child you have the honor of changing fifty trillion times a day?

According to some bloke on the internet, so it must have been true, this was a true prize and much sought after. Worth a bloody fortune too, by the seems of it. The older the dragon, the more potent it was.

What caught my eye was the various treatments for it. Fresh, it was hard like a pellet, yet could be broken up easily enough, but the author recommended drying it out somewhere warm, and that was when the magic truly happened.

It would become firm, then crystallize, and resemble just that—a crystal. Turning from dark brown to utterly black, and it would grow and double in size. Once it had lost all traces of moisture, it would be as hard as crystal, duh, and could be consumed in any number of ways. You could crunch it if you didn't value your mouth or throat as it was sharp as glass, or you could crush it in a pestle and mortar and consume the powder any way you wanted.

There was a warning. The power you got was temporary. Sometimes hours, sometimes days, again tied to the age of the dragon. The older the dragon, the rarer the poo, the longer it would continue working.

Get some dragon poo from one a thousand years old and it would give you generous powers that would last out your lifetime, and we were talking Necro lifespans here.

"What you doing?" asked Phage with a mischievous smile.

I slammed the laptop shut and said, "Checking my email. How's Jen?"

"Moaning about not being able to wear jeans. But she's fine. Sorry I fell asleep last night. I missed our first proper night in bed together." She kissed my cheek.

"Hey, we have the rest of our lives, right?"

We exchanged a look; we both knew this could be our last few days together. "We do. Jen's like a bottle of pop now. She's asking a million questions. I mean, we can't leave it like this, can we? She wants to know if she's immortal, and in the next breath she's asking if we can go shopping, seeing as she isn't going to school. And she asked if she can have more dragon poo when she's older. And how old are we? And will Woofer die, and all sorts."

"Woofer will die," came the dour moan of my faithful companion. "But Woofer might not die if he eats Tyr poo. Will Woofer live forever then? Be with Soph and Phage and Jen always?"

"He wants to know if he'll be immortal if he eats Tyr's poo," I told Phage.

"We don't know, Woofer. We'll find out, okay?" Phage told him kindly.

Woofer skulked off with his tail down.

"Okay, I read some of it. It said you take on the dragon's magic, their abilities, or some of it. But the older they are, or the more mature, on their way to adulthood, the longer the effects last. If you eat the poo of an old dragon, the effects last as long as you do."

"What will they be?"

"Some of what the dragon can do. I'm guessing immortality, repairing damage to your body, maybe going invisible. Tyr can do that already. Damn, has Jen been invisible?"

"I didn't see her do it." Phage laughed at her own joke. I just groaned. She leaned in close and whispered. "So, if we get some very old dragon poo, Woofer could become immortal?"

"I guess. I think so. But what if he ends up breathing fire and eating Necros? Or puking acid? That's a pretty hefty side effect."

"We need to look into this. I can't even believe we're having this conversation. It's poo!"

"Yeah, haha, nuts. Phage, we need to talk, I mean properly talk. We need to decide what to do. We have to go. We need to pack and we need to leave. Will Peth stay and look after Jen? Of course she will. Sorry, she already said. Ugh, I am knackered."

"Go and have a doze. You look awful. And Soph, I'm sorry you had to do that yesterday. I truly am. But he deserved it."

"Yeah, maybe," I grumbled, then headed for the living room and to the sanctuary of my recliner. I was absolutely exhausted and it wasn't even ten AM.

The Cat Acts Nice

I sank into my recliner after evicting an idiot dwarf by means of multitudinous and creative swear words, then sighed with contentment. My head was spinning. Should I have stayed in hospital? How had my life gone from shit to nightmare within a day? Bloody mothers-in-law everywhere, and that was never good. She could make a troll run with a stare, let alone a poor guy with a lot on his plate.

As my eyes closed, I felt a sinister presence turn the room cold. It was like all fun and laughter was expelled, or simply ran off looking for a brighter future, and then I felt the source of the energy drain settle in my lap. My heavy lids lifted and there was Mr. Wonderful, purring contentedly as he kneaded my legs with his paws, scagging my jeans and generally having a great time.

"Hey, why do you do that?" I asked, wondering if maybe this time I'd get an answer.

"To make it more comfortable," he sighed, like it was obvious.

"But it's my legs. You can't mold them into another shape."

"Just go with it," he said dreamily, his entire body vibrating as the rumble from deep within picked up pace.

"Okay. So, to what do I owe the dubious honor?"

"It's that woman. She doesn't like me."

"What? No, seriously?" I struggled to keep a straight face.

Mr. Wonderful nodded his cute little head; his tiny pink tongue poked out as he thought about things. "I think I intimidate her, so she's mean to me. All I did was rub against her legs and I might have been saying I owned her, but only because she was in my house."

"Yeah, some people are just funny like that. What can you do? Just get on with your life, I guess."

"Do you like me?" He studied me with eyes that knew so much, yet knew so little. His cat brain was wired so differently to any other creature I had ever encountered, I simply could not fathom it, or him.

"Course I do," I said solemnly, not even a twitch of my mouth.

"See, that's right. Of course you do. Why wouldn't you? But Peth, she really isn't interested. Weird."

"Yeah, especially as you are so interested in everyone else and care so much about their feelings."

Mr. Wonderful rubbed a lazy paw over his head and nodded sagely. His eyes began to close, then they snapped open and he glared at me. "Are you being funny?"

"No, of course not." I covered my mouth with my hand, as the giggles were building, but he nodded again, closed his eyes, and stilled.

He was such a peculiar animal. Utterly indifferent to anyone or anything else, with a deep-seated belief in his own superiority, and yet, at times like this, it was almost like he cared. How long had he been with me now? Over half a century. Fifty-seven years in total, from when he was a teeny tiny kitten and as cute as cute can be.

It was obvious immediately he wasn't a normal cat. He was too white, too clean even for a cat, and way too smart. He was also sitting on top of a Rottweiler's head and the poor dog was as still as the troll in the garden, his fear was so deep. I should have known better than to take the cat off the owner's hands. If anyone offers you free pussy, there are always strings attached. Always. I've paid for it ever since.

Mr. Wonderful was fearless, that was the problem. Being immortal makes you that way. As to how he has infinite lives, I never discovered. Some creatures, like some humans, are simply born that way. Part of the Necroverse whether they like it or not, same as the rest of us.

With the dread of a lifetime of Mr. Wonderful's indifference hanging over me, I nevertheless nodded off and for a while there was peace. Just a guy in his recliner with his rumbling cat curled up in his lap. I could almost believe I was a normal human being. Almost.

Mr. Wonderful was gone when I finally stirred. He'd left the guts of a mouse smeared over my leg as a thank you. Phage smiled, and used a rag to scoop it up, then patted me on the head and asked, "Nice sleep?"

I yawned and said, "Yeah, and thanks for the clean-up. You're too good to me."

"Don't I know it. As long as you do too. Fancy a cuppa? Maybe a stroll in the garden? Just the two of us?"

"Definitely. Where is everyone?"

"Mother and Jen are upstairs in her room. She's helping Jen's leg repair faster. Just a few whispers now she's recovered from last night's work."

"Great, that's great. I just need a pee, then I'll be right there." After doing the necessary, as even perfect husbands and fathers need to wee, I put on my boots and coat and found Phage in the garden. She passed me a steaming mug of sweet tea and I drank gratefully. I hadn't realized how thirsty I was.

"How are you holding up?" asked Phage.

I shrugged. "I'm fine, I guess. Tired, hurt a bit, but I'm more concerned about Jen than anything. Can't believe she's been reading about all this on the internet! Damn computers."

"There's no getting away from it now. It's part of life. It's always been part of mine. Us youngsters don't remember a time before the web."

"You missed a lot. But so did we. What are we going to do? She knows about Necros, more than I thought. And now this with the poo. I can't even believe it's a thing."

"She's young and inquisitive. It was bound to happen. At least she hasn't done anything daft. She's a smart girl. We'll have to tell her certain things when we get back, and Soph, we will get back. Come home. I know you could do without this, but we don't have a choice. The sooner we get going, the sooner we'll be home. We need to go. Either today, or tomorrow at the latest. Jen's going to be so annoyed with us. You've been home a day, and she didn't even get to see you yesterday. She's only had a few hours with you. And now we're leaving her."

"Yeah, with Peth."

"Do you have a better idea? At least with Mother we know she'll be safe. Either here or with the other witches."

"I think here will be fine. I hope it will, at least." I drained my tea and tried to think clearly, but my head was fuzzy and the stress of my daughter being hurt left me jittery and uncomfortable. "Ugh, I can't think. Can't seem to get going."

"It's because you aren't well yet. And I'm sorry about last night. I shouldn't have told you to do that. Was it awful?"

"I killed a man for hurting our daughter. He wasn't a nice guy, but yes, it was awful. It always is. But it's done. Come on, show me what our mental neighbor's been up to now. I need something to take my mind off things before we come up with a plan."

Phage grinned mischievously at me. "Oh, you're going to love it. While you were away he's been out there every day, even in the snow. He's getting grumpier too."

"Haha, now that I can't believe. He maxed out on grump years ago. It's not possible to get more miserable than Job."

"Wanna bet? Come on." We left our mugs beside the troll, then hand in hand we wandered down our land, following footsteps in the snow. We passed the zoo, then the barns and various buildings to the fence line of the far paddock. A strange beast stuck its ugly claws above the treetops in our friendly neighbor's wilderness.

"Damn, it's grown a lot. I didn't look properly yesterday or this morning, but it's got a lot bigger, hasn't it?"

"Yeah, and look, he's up there." Phage pointed and I could just about make out a tiny figure hanging precariously from a beam of some sort. "I've even gone over while he's working but he wouldn't let me near. Shouted at me and said he'd eat the dog if I trespassed again."

"Haha, he's such a kidder. He loves Woofer really. Who could resist the cute guy?"

"Oh yes, he was definitely kidding. Not." Phage winked. She liked Job, same as I did. In that way you like Marmite even though everyone knows it's actually utterly gross and the best marketing gimmick in history for what is basically stuff to be thrown away.

As we giggled and peered through the overgrown hedge, disturbed snow fell onto our heads, making us laugh more. Funny how we always knew what the best thing to do was to change our mood. We really were made for each other.

Phage wobbled a prickly hawthorn branch and snow turned the world white. She smiled, full of mischief, and I loved her even more than ever. Then a picture of her killing a stranger entered my head and the two images simply would not compute. Was she looking at me the same way? I shook the snow and the image away because now wasn't the time for darkness. Now was the time for light and getting shouted at by your neighbor.

We clambered over the fence, careful of the rotting posts I really needed to replace one of these days, and then we traipsed through the barren meadows. The flowers were long gone, just rotting under the dusting of snow. It wasn't hard to pick out Job's progress; he'd clearly been back and forth several times today and a muddy path was the result. We cut across the field to the track, then followed the trail of nuts and bolts, timber scraps, several rusty saws, five hammers, and more empty beer bottles than could possibly be safe for someone working at such height or even on the ground if he had a hammer left.

As we got closer to the copse of trees, we slowed, then stopped and marveled at the monstrosity. There was no logic to it, no symmetry. Girders jutted, half-finished platforms seemed to serve no other purpose than to confuse you, and huge telegraph poles pointed accusingly at the wintry sky as if to say it was the world's fault, not Job's.

"He's crazy." I shook my head in dismay. He must have lost the plot entirely; that was the only explanation.

"I don't think so. He knows exactly what he's doing." Phage squinted, then shielded her eyes against the snow glare as we studied the impossible build together. The more I looked, the more it made sense somehow. A cohesive whole when at first there seemed no rhyme nor reason to it. Maybe he did have a plan.

"Come on, let's go say hello. Maybe this time he'll take pity on us and put us out of our misery." I took Phage's hand and we moved cautiously to the edge of the woods.

"Call him then," she said.

"You call him. He likes you more."

"Does not. Are you scared?" she chided.

"Yes." I smiled, but I wasn't really joking. "Aw, bugger it. Job, can we come and have a look?" I shouted into the woods.

"Who's that?" he called down from somewhere up high.

"It's Soph and Phage. I'm back."

"Wait there. Don't come into the woods. You're trespassing. Fuck." Something clanged as it fell through the structure, hopefully not Job. We stepped back to the edge of the trees and waited while the sweaty old man swore his way towards us.

"What?" A slim harness was pulled tight around his crotch then fastened at the waist. An impressive collection of carabiners were attached to his belt, and thick rope coiled over his shoulder. He finished his beer and threw the bottle into a pile.

"What ya doin'?" I asked, grinning.

"Having a fucking tea party. Would you like to come?"

"Come on, what are you building in here? I've been gone for months and you still haven't finished. What's the deal?"

"I told you, and you, hello Phage, that you'll have to wait. It isn't finished. Just a little while longer."

"No teaser? No hint?" asked Phage, batting her eyelids.

"Fuck off." Her womanly charms were lost on Job. He turned serious, more serious than usual, and asked me, "How are you doing? Hear you got your ass kicked."

"I'm okay. It's good to be home. But listen, while we're here, I want to let you know that we're both going to be away for a few days. Either from tonight or tomorrow. Peth is here to look after Jen, but can you listen out, just in case?"

"Hell, you're leaving her with that woman? No offense, Phage."

"None taken. It won't be for long. We have to go. And Jen got run over yesterday, hence why Mother is here."

"Shit! Is she okay?"

"She's on the mend. But it was nasty. She'll be fine, but will you just listen out? Any problems, Peth should be able to handle things. But you know we worry."

"Yeah, I'll check on 'em. Hope you got the bugger that hurt Jen."

"I got him."

"Good. Now, where you going?" Job frowned while the mental gears clicked, then he said, "Fuck. It's your birthday, right? Happy fucking birthday. There's only one reason you'd both be going away. That sucks. I had one like that once. It was a bastard nightmare. Absolute twistfuck of a crazy-ass few days. Never saw the missus like that before. It was a real eye-opener. I remember once it was finished, we couldn't keep our hands off each other. We got with it on a—"

"We get the idea. And yeah, it's not something we're looking forward to, but there's no choice."

"Nope, absolutely none," he said with grim delight. "Well, have fun. Try not to die, and if you do, can I have your stuff?"

"No, you bloody can't. And this better be finished when we get home. You wily old bugger."

"It'll be ready when it's ready. Now get the fuck off my land." Job smiled like the devil he undoubtedly was, then yanked on his harness and stormed back off into the woods, calling the trees names as he went.

"Well, that was pointless," I told Phage.

"Always is, but visiting Job always cheers me up, as it makes me grateful for my lovely hunk of man meat." She pinched my bum playfully and I laughed.

She was right, because no matter how bad you thought you had it, you always knew there was someone more miserable than you after a chat with Job.

Always Something

As we wandered back up the land then into the garden, I couldn't help but stop Phage and just kiss her. Just because I wanted to.

"What was that for?"

"Because you're my wife and I love you. And because I'm happy. Happy to be here with you and Jen. I know I can be grumpy, but I honestly am blessed to have you both. That scared me yesterday, I know you too. I can't imagine life without her."

"Neither can I. We won't lose her. She's a fighter."

"That's the problem. She'll have to be."

Whrump!

The unmistakable sound of a shotgun being fired reverberated around our sweet slice of paradise. Birds flew from bare branches, the animals complained from their warm nests. The echo bounced off the hedges, the buildings and the houses, then was sucked up by the snow, deadening the dreadful signal of misadventure.

"Where did that come from?" whispered Phage, ducked down low behind the troll, same as me.

"I think it was from Mrs. O'Donnell's. She's probably after rats again. Bloody hell, haha, scared me half to death. I can't take any more excitement at the moment."

"She needs to warn us before she starts shooting that bloody thing. What if she hits one of us?"

"Then I'll go and tell her off," I laughed, the relief palpable. "I'll pop around and have a word. Just make sure she's okay." I stood and Phage joined me.

Whrump!

There it was again.

Birds just beginning to perch again scattered once more. We took cover out of instinct but smiled, feeling foolish as we got to our feet.

"She's a bloody menace. That sounded like it was inside the house. You go and tell Jen not to worry, I'll check on Mrs. O'Donnell."

Phage nodded and headed towards the house, then stopped and came back. "What if it's burglars?" she whispered.

"Then I'll kick their asses."

"Maybe I should come."

"And what if there are burglars? Although you don't get many in the middle of the day. When it's been snowing."

"Then *I'll* kick their asses." Phage held up a hand for a high five.

"That was crap. You don't deserve one," I told her.

Phage wiggled her eyebrows. "Don't leave me hanging."

With a sigh, I slapped palms with my wife then watched her go inside. Wondering what madness our aging neighbor was up to, I figured it best to make a sneaky approach just in case there was any actual bother. Not that I expected there to be. But knowing my luck, there could be a team of daemons dancing on her wrinkly head.

I sprinted back down the garden, took a right past the Necropub, longing for a beer now, then ducked around a corner into a neglected part of our land and wriggled through the hawthorn. I got scratched to buggery, which did nothing to improve my souring mood.

Sweet Old Ladies

Mrs. O'Donnell's place was a weird setup, same as all our properties. We hit each other's land at odd angles, which meant there was privacy and space between the actual houses. Her home was across a scrappy paddock where geese caused carnage, then there was her meticulous garden that backed onto ours, and then her quaint cottage. It was years since I'd been inside, but it was your typical old lady's country abode, complete with farmhouse kitchen, low ceilings, more wooden beams than a medium-sized forest could support, and rammed full of a lifetime's worth of ornaments, furniture, and what have you.

Our neighbor had been living in the country for seventy years but still had an Irish twang, and as far as I could recall she'd resided in this house for nigh on twenty years. Longer than us, but not an eternity either.

I dashed past the geese—who were none too happy about my sudden appearance, and they let me know it— then through a gate into her bare garden. It was so different to the blaring colors of summer, as she did like her bedding plants no matter that she was getting older and the work was becoming too much. Mrs. O'Donnell refused to give up, although she had slowed down over the years, relying on a little help to keep the lawn in good shape. She preferred to focus on weeding and slug control, a pastime she took rather too much delight in.

I moved fast, but not too fast as the grass was slippery and the last thing I wanted was to get soaked. At the back of the house, I stepped onto the patio outside a small lean-to where she kept the washing machine and various odds and ends. After a quick listen, I yanked open the door.

"Fuck!" It sounded like she was being marauded by a herd of buffalo. Furniture snapped, ornaments, plates, or cutlery or something made a terrible racket as it smashed into floors and walls. What the hell was going on? The general impression was full-on warfare. Burglars then? Attacking a defenseless old lady? Fuckers. We'd soon sort that out. Shouldn't be too much trouble, especially if she had a shotgun.

I entered the lean-to, then through the door into her kitchen. Mrs. O'Donnell's back was to me, her tiny frame topped by a head of silver hair in tight curls. She threw a saucepan at a young man in his late twenties or early thirties and then she screamed, surprisingly strongly and with utter menace, before launching at the guy with a frying pan and slamming him across the side of the head. The handle broke off the pan and it clattered to the tiles as the intruder shook his head then swiped at her with a large folding knife.

I gasped, believing I was too late, but my gossiping neighbor stepped deftly aside and brought her arm down on the guy's forearm with a smart chop. She followed up with a left-hand jab to his nose. Cartilage crunched, a sound I was all-too-familiar with, having broken more noses than I could count over the years. My own included.

He grunted, but the wildness was on him. With blood pouring, he punched out and caught the dear old lady with a strong right hook. Her neck snapped back and her head careened sideways into a wall cupboard. She bounced off, then wailed and just charged straight at the guy, somehow pinning the knife arm as she tore at his face with her teeth like a rabid dog.

What. The. Fuck. Was. Going. On?

I was stunned not only by the ferocity, but by the obvious skills she had. She did what I would have done: Read the man's body language, anticipate his moves, never fall for the obvious. Mrs. O'Donnell flowed fluidly with grace, surprising agility, and some inhuman strength.

I inched forward, not wanting to distract my friend and neighbor, and as I checked on her from behind, actually looked properly, it was as though she'd grown a good six inches. Gone was the rounded back, the skinny shoulders, and the flat arse. She was slender but toned and fit, with a body more akin to someone half her age. It wasn't her. Maybe her daughter? I hadn't seen her for many years, and they did look alike, but what was with the hair? Even as I thought it, the silver mop of curls shimmered and shook out, revealing pale blond, almost white locks in loose ringlets that hung past her shoulders.

As I tried to process this, and trust me, it did not compute, the "burglar" saw me and panicked. He charged out of the room then banged about, I assumed in the living room.

"Mrs. O'Donnell?" I asked.

"Call me Shae," she said as she whipped her head around, a punch only just halted.

"What the hell?" It was her, but not her. Tall, proud, sleek, and beautiful. With strange green eyes, a button nose, dimples, and cheeks like soft bread rolls, pale and rounded.

"We might need a chat later, Soph, but for now, can you help me kill this bastard? I'm a little out of practice, and the cold plays havoc with my joints. Haha." Mrs. O'Donnell, apparently Shae, cackled as she ran after the man she had been giving a pounding to. The shotgun went off.

"Shae, you okay?" I shouted as I eased to the doorway and poked my head around.

"Fine. Haha, he's a feisty one." She turned and smiled, then winked salaciously before she ran off into the living room. It was never a word I'd ever imagined using to describe the old lady!

"I'll kill you, you mad bitch," shouted the intruder, his voice less than confident, but a hundred percent pissed-off.

"I've fought better than you, boy. Much better. You picked the wrong fucking granny to mess with."

I followed them, on auto-pilot now. Explanations could come later. This was my friend and she might, *might*, need my help.

The kid was fumbling with the shotgun and a box of ammo, but he was out of time. Shae crouched, then leapt at him with a roar of primal rage. She smacked into his torso and they tumbled back into the TV, then flipped over onto the smashed screen on top of the old pine stand. She was wild, punching and tearing at his head, utterly manic and fully consumed with bloodlust.

The lad was all arms and legs, hitting and kicking anything he could, but neither of them was doing much damage as they were too close, too in each other's faces.

I scoured the room, then pulled an old-fashioned floor lamp's cable from the socket, broke the lead from the base, and kicked crap out of my way as I took the few steps needed to cross the room.

As Shae rolled off the man, I stepped up to take her place and deftly looped the wire around his neck several times.

Muscles strained, veins popped, and the dude goggled as his eyes bugged out and his shaved head turned purple. A fat tongue stuck out as he hissed while batting at my arms feebly.

I yanked back hard and fast. The cable cut deep into his throat but didn't break the skin, but he was gasping now, head so crimson I expected it to pop. He chopped at my arms again and again, and I was losing my grip so I leaned back then braced my feet against the broken cabinet and tugged for all I was worth as he choked to death.

He fumbled about with his right hand then caught his knife and slashed down onto the cable. It frayed and I fell backwards onto my arse. With a scream so raw and full of rage it made me shudder, the man kicked me in the head, rolled off the stand, then swung out wildly and half-blind in sweeping arcs to clear some space.

As I scrambled back, the man howled. At first I believed in anger and frustration, and a lot of pain, but it was the cry of a shifter. He morphed into something obscene. He was neither one thing nor another. A true beast. The redness of his head spread over his entire body as hair sprouted until he resembled a patchy red dog but with scales and bird talons and the teeth of a boar. Two tusks tore through his jaw and when he screamed this time it was obvious why. He was an animorph of the most unfortunate kind. Too young to have mastery, too unbalanced to be a single creature, and definitely inexperienced. Beyond an amateur, this guy had probably only changed a few times in his life and had no clue how to control it.

A failure of the Necroverse. An unfortunate who would never survive.

I hurried to my feet then stepped away from the poor soul as he continued to shift, never settling.

"You okay?" I asked Shae.

"Fine. A few cuts and bruises. Sorry about this, it was somewhat unexpected. Haha. Damn, never had one come after me before. You?"

"What? I don't understand."

"The Necronotes. He's got one with my name on it. The bastards sent him to kill me. Well, maybe not. Poor sod, looks like they sent him so I'd do their dirty work for them. The wankers."

"No. Wait!" But it was too late.

Shae skirted around the animal, and just as the eyes snapped open and the feral beast tensed to attack, her eyes turned cold, her jaw tensed, and she snatched up the fallen knife and stabbed it straight into the abomination's throat.

Shae jumped back, the knife left embedded. For several seconds, the poor thing thrashed about wildly, clawing at the knife as the blood flowed and life seeped away. He managed to grip it and tugged it free with a spray of red mist that covered Shae.

The knife dropped to the patterned carpet, the body slumped sideways, and the lad changed back to human form. A naked, skinny man-boy covered in scars, wounds fresh and old. I could see his ribs through taut, mottled skin.

Piss and shit streamed from between legs criss-crossed with scars, injuries no doubt inflicted on himself when in the throes of shifting.

"Look at the mess, and on my rug too. I'll never get the stains out. Tea towels, I need tea towels. Oh, and my doilies. They were valuable. Had them for the longest time." Shae wandered off then returned with an armful of neatly folded tea towels. She stood there, unmoving, staring at the corpse, the mess the room was in, the dark, stinking patch beneath the body of a broken boy who never stood a chance.

The tea towels fell to the floor, Shae hung her head, and her shoulders sagged. She sobbed. Great, heaving sobs. She cried for the boy, for herself, for all us Necros.

"Look what we do to each other. Look at what we've become. I'm more of a monster than he ever was, or ever would be. Fucking doilies."

I wrapped her in my arms and let her cry it out.

It took a long time.

I placed a mug of strong tea in front of Shae, then popped outside and called Phage. I spared her the details, told her everything was fine and I was just having a cuppa with Mrs. O'Donnell and would be back soon. She asked about the shotgun, so I told her it was just her putting a poorly goose out of its misery. It sounded lame even to me, but Phage didn't question it. Country folk get up to all sorts —you only have to see our other neighbor to know that's the case.

Back inside, I sank into a chair and sipped my tea while keeping my eyes on Shae.

"So, anything you want to tell me?" I asked, unable to stop my smile.

"No," she said gruffly, sounding more like the woman I believed I'd lived next to for so many years.

"No? Nothing?"

"Maybe a thing or two," she said, her smile weak. Sadness was all that remained.

"I can't believe all these years and you had us fooled. Even Phage. Even Peth. Damn, you must be good to be able to put up a veil like that. They'll be so pissed you tricked them."

"I'm good at what I do. Had a lot of practice. I like it here, Soph. I like my quiet life. I hardly see anybody, so it's easy enough to muster the magic to veil myself when I have a chat with you over the fence. Mostly I'm on my own, you know that, so it's no problem. I store it up, then use the veil when I need to."

"Even so, it's impressive. You been doing it a long time, eh?"

"A very long time. I'm an old woman, Soph. Much older than you."

"You don't know how old I am. How could you?"

"Maybe not the exact date, but close enough. I've been around. I wasn't always an old lady in a cottage. I know the stories about you from way back. I am part of the Necroverse. I was old before you were born. I have lived countless lives in endless guises, moved here, there, and everywhere. Had husbands and children and lost so many. I know more about you than you might believe."

"Damn, just how old are you?"

"Old enough. Old and tired. I know your name. I knew it the day you moved here, with Phage. I know of Peth and her sisters, and what they do. I understand so much but know so little. And through it all, the notes endure. Always the notes. Always."

"Yeah, always the notes."

"You are nice neighbors, and I like living here. I decided to stay as long as I could. Soon it will be time to move on, but I'll remain as long as I am able. Before there are too many questions. The veil helps, but you can only be an old woman for so long before it gets too complicated. The digital age doesn't make it easier. It makes it so much harder."

"I bet. Everything's recorded. All your details, all the records, date of birth, the lot."

"Yes, so you have to move on eventually. And then everything gets miraculously updated. Changed, and you can start again. I don't know how they know, but they always do it. I decided to move, so I can have another go at aging, and just like that I get my new paperwork, my online trail is cold, and my birth date has changed. New identification, new numbers, all of it. It's so complicated. How do they do it?"

"Buggered if I know. But listen, how do you know about us? How did you know we were Necros? I mean, yeah, I get it, Necros can usually tell each other, but the details? Phage and Peth?"

"Because I've been around, I told you. I know things. I remember the names of so many like us. And Soph?"

"Yeah?"

"When you have a dumb unicorn always breaking windows, and a dragon in a barn, and all those other strange creatures, it does make it rather obvious." Shae patted my arm in a maternal way and smiled weakly.

"Haha, guess that would give it away. So, you can see them as they truly are? Sorry, duh, course you can. Okay, so what's with the young lad? Poor kid, that's no way to go. And sorry, I just couldn't do it. I've had so much death lately, so much. I felt sorry for him. Just couldn't kill the poor creature. No, not a creature, a young man. A broken young man."

"He came for me. I am sorry, truly I am, but it was him or me. How do we decide, Soph? How do we know what's right? Should I have let him kill me? His life for mine? I don't want to die, but I hate this killing. You know what the worst thing is?"

"I do. But tell me anyway. Just so I know it isn't me."

"It's that I can do it at all. I took the life of a poor, broken boy who didn't want to hurt me, not really, and I did it so I could survive. I can kill with ease, and that, more than anything, tells me I am no good."

"It's what they made us. It's what we've become."

"Monsters. Every year I kill, every year I question myself. If it was right, if they should have died. Every damn year for century after century. And now it seems my time is short. That I have been marked. It's the way of it. Only the notes endure."

"Will you stop fucking saying that! Everyone always says that. Fuck!" I banged my fist onto the table; the mugs jumped. She turned away. "Sorry. But it's that damn saying. I hate it. Christ, yesterday Jen nearly died, now this. Oh, and just so you know, Phage and I are going on a little jolly. She got her note, and it had both our names on it. I can't believe all this, in a single bloody day. It's too much."

"Jen? Is she alright? What happened? And I'm sorry about the note. Had a few of those over the years. Watch yourself, Soph. You are, what do they say now, leveling up?"

"Leveling up? Ha, more like sinking down. Jen's fine. Peth is here to look after her. I killed the man that knocked her over. Another death. Look, I have to go. I need to clear my head. You going to be okay?"

"I always am. I'll carry on. First I'll have a weep, then question my sorry existence, then I'll return to being the sweet, foul-mouthed old lady you gossip with over the fence."

"You don't need to pretend for us. We've got a lot to tell Jen, but soon we'll explain a little more about all this, then you can be whoever you want to be." I nodded to this woman, this stranger, then I left her to her misery.

The world was white outside. A fresh blanket of snow had fallen, and that special stillness that came with it wrapped the world in peace. I stood in the garden of my friend and tried to suck some of that peace inside my raging mind.

I was there until I was numb, but I found no solace, only misery.

Lunch Time

"I made sandwiches," said Phage, smiling sweetly as I entered the kitchen through the back door.

"Great," I grunted, as I moved fast through the room, heading to get cleaned up.

"Soph? What's wrong?"

"Trust me, you do not want to know. Not now. Everything's fine, but I need to wash up. Where's Jen?"

"Just finishing up with Mother. They'll be down soon. Look at your face, and your hands. Is that blood?"

"Yes. It's a long story for something that didn't take much time, but everything's okay."

"Was it a burglar then?"

"You could say that. Later, okay?"

"Sure, as long as you're alright?"

"I'm hanging in there by the skin of my teeth. Be back in a jiffy. Just need to get to the bathroom." I left Phage to it while I tried to wash away the filth. It never came off. No matter how hard I tried, I could never escape the foulness. It went more than skin deep now. It infected me. Infected us all.

Where the hell had my good mood gone? Why couldn't I keep the joy I felt only yesterday when I woke up in my own bed and had months of relaxation to look forward to? Mental wounds from Liverpool had hardly begun to heal, and now this? I wanted to rage, tear everything down. Burn it. Destroy it all. Rip the corrupted soul out of this life and throw it into a raging furnace. Slam the door shut on it for good.

But I couldn't, so I scrubbed my hands, plastered a smile on my face, and went to have sandwiches with my family instead.

Jen was bubbly and very excited about missing school, although she couldn't wait to get back so her friends could write on her cast. She pouted when Peth broke the news to her that it would be off tomorrow, and even now it was merely a precaution. Seemed this witch bitch really was a dab hand with the whispers when it came to broken bones.

Phage was quiet, same as me, and Peth was her usual weird self. Her forked tongue made her lisp somewhat when she spoke, and combined with the eyes, I always thought of her as like a snake. Although snake eyes are vertical, if I've got my biology correct.

After we'd finished lunch and cleaned up the kitchen, Peth excused herself and left the three of us alone. I nodded my thanks to her and she nodded back—I hated it when she was nice and understanding. That wasn't her at all.

"Okay, I think we need to have a little chat," I told Jen.

"About time."

"But we can't tell you everything," said Phage.

"No, there is a lot you mustn't know until you are older."

"How old? Thirteen?"

"Older. Probably. Look, Jen, you're young and have your whole life ahead of you, and like I already said, at least I think I did, you can live a very long time."

"Haha. Yeah. Um, were you serious?"

"Your father is three hundred and forty years old," Phage told her.

"No way. That's unreal!"

"Actually, I'm three hundred and forty-four. Born July seventeenth. Don't forget. I want presents."

"So, that means you were born... Um, hang on. Sixteen ninety. Haha, that is so crazy. So, all those times you used to go on about remembering when it was just horses, no cars, you weren't even joking? About there not being computers and no electricity? That was true?"

"Yep, 'fraid so, kiddo. Your dad's an old, old man. I've seen so much, done even more, and trust me, I know we keep saying it's like going back in time with these cuts and quotas and restrictions and what have you, but it is still very much the modern age. Especially when you remember a time when people threw their toilet waste out of the window into the street."

"Shut up!"

"It's true. But your Mum's not old. She's too pretty to be old. But she is older than you think by a few years. She's forty-eight, but likes to remain looking early thirties."

"Thirty-five. I chose thirty-five. Although that's sweet of you." Phage winked.

"Is this a joke? I know Tyr is kinda immortal, and sorry again about the poo thing, but we can really live for a long time? Wow! So, how old's Grandma?"

"You'll have to ask her that one. Um, how old is she?" I asked Phage.

"You were right, you'll have to ask her. Even I don't know. But I think it's maybe double Soph's age, could be more. Your Grandmother is a very powerful witch, can do many wondrous things, but she also likes to dabble in very dangerous areas of magic. Not anything you should ever get involved in. It's very risky."

"So she really is a witch? I knew she was, and maybe you too, Mum, but this just makes it properly real. Why haven't we spoken about this before?"

"Honey, you're eleven. You're young, still innocent, and we wanted to keep it that way." I kissed the top of her head; she grinned sheepishly.

"Let's start with what you do know, or what we think you know. Tyr. Do you know what he's done over recent years to grow so much?" asked Phage.

"He said he killed people. And drank their blood, then took on their powers. So he can be invisible now, and he showed me he can turn into this cute, scruffy dog. And he can breathe fire and belch acid, but I haven't seen the acid."

"That's all true," I told her. "Tyr killed, and if he kills what I believe you know is called a Necro, then he takes their abilities. He executed a shifter, now he can become that animal. He can even look like the men he killed. And yes, he belches acid. I learned a lot from an old man before I was in the hospital, and Tyr has grown faster than he really should, but it confirmed the fact that he is extremely dangerous. I know I've told you this before, but this is beyond important, so I'm going to tell you again. If dragons aren't with their owners a lot, they won't listen to a word they say. You must keep the bond with him, or he will be utterly wild. He scared me. He was lost to bloodlust, and I thought, just for a moment, he was going to turn on me. I warned him, told him I was his master and if he ever scared me he would be banished, never see us again. You must be firm with him if he needs it. You must always be in charge. In control. Understand?"

"Yes. Absolutely."

"Tyr will be faithful. He loves you very much. In thousands of years he will want to be alone, so will go off and sleep for centuries, become lost to us, but that's not for a very long time. Um, let me see. You know about Bernard and Kayin, about all the other animals, and you can talk to them. Anything else you can do?"

"I don't think so. What might I be able to do?"

"Shift, duplicate yourself. Your mother can do that. Turn into something strange. And we can both do this thing we call morphing. You can travel from one place to another without it taking hardly any time. You kind of turn into little bits, tiny pieces, and travel through the air, through objects, walls, anything. The witches are very good at it."

"No way! That is beyond cool. You guys are awesome. Can I try? Just like Woofer did? That's what he did, right? He ate Tyr's poo and he got some magic."

"Yes, but Tyr can't do that, so I'm not really sure how Woofer got the ability."

"Don't you see?" said Jen. "He got magic. He used it how he wanted. He copied you."

"Yeah, I guess. See, this is the thing with being a Necro. It doesn't automatically mean you have all the answers. We don't understand half of what this all is. As you get older, you will discover what you are capable of. It should start when you hit puberty properly, in a few years. Until then, enjoy being young and free. There will be lots of practice, a ton of training, and a lot of hurt. Because, be warned, these abilities come at a price. A high one. It hurts like hell to morph, even now for me, even for your grandmother. But when you are young and first learning, man, you will not believe the agony."

"I can take it," Jen said, defiant.

"Haha, I don't doubt it. You are one tough young lady. Um, so, is that it? Gosh, that wasn't so bad. Haha, I was dreading this." I turned to Phage. "Anything else?"

"I don't think so. Not now, anyway. The main thing is that you will change a lot, things will happen, but you have our support. It wasn't like that for us. We had a very different upbringing to you. Your father was sent away at about your age, to a special school where Necro children were trained hard, and it wasn't nice. I lived with your grandmother, and it was not a conventional upbringing. You have us, a home, your animals, and we will do whatever we can to ensure you cope. But you must trust our judgment. Understand?"

"Sure, Mum. And Dad?"

"Hmm?"

"You don't look a day over three hundred." Jen pecked me on the cheek, her eyes dancing like her mother's.

"Thanks. I think. Okay, so, you good? You understand everything so far? You sure you are alright after yesterday? That gave us such a shock. We thought we'd lost our little girl."

"Not so little any more." Jen stood and clenched her fists, then closed her eyes and hissed as her face turned red.

"What you doing?" I asked.

"Trying to morph. But it isn't working."

"Give it ten years, then try again," I laughed. Hoping she would, knowing she wouldn't.

"It was worth a try. Now, why do you get hurt every year? What are Necronotes? And do you really kill people?"

I groaned. It was going so well too.

"Why do you think we kill people?" asked Phage.

"Mum, I meant Dad, of course. Silly. Do you, Dad?"

"Why on earth would you think that?" I tried to sound light-hearted, but I wasn't sure if I pulled it off.

"Because of what Tyr said. That he killed men, killed a man years ago, a Necro, and the other month he fed, but said he thought you killed him. Erm, maybe. No, wait. Ah, that's it. Sorry, he killed them both. I think. Sometimes it's hard to tell with Tyr."

"Let's just say that Tyr likes to exaggerate. But he fed on people who died, okay? Don't go looking into this too much, as you won't like everything you discover. Be patient, that's all we ask. I know this is overwhelming. It's a lot more to take in than finding you can talk to animals. You have a very long life ahead, so it's doubly important that you are careful. Think of it. You could live for hundreds and hundreds of years like me. Imagine what the future will be like."

"It's gonna be awesome. I bet I'll have a jet-pack and be able to do gaming by closing my eyes and using my implant. I'll be able to morph everywhere in the world and maybe there will be spaceships again and we can go on holiday to Mars. How cool would that be?"

"Very cool. Right, this has been a very long day so far for everyone. Let's have some down time and go play in the snow. I don't know about you, but I'm in desperate need of a carrot."

"Huh? Oh, is that a Necro thing?"

"No, it's for the snowman we're gonna build. Haha."

"Dad!" Jen hugged me tight, then her mother. She hobbled off to go get her coat and to find Peth.

"That went better than expected," said Phage, clearly relieved.

"Sure did. Damn, we need to tell her we have to go away. First thing in the morning, we'll go then."

"Yes, let's have a nice relaxing evening together. Light the stove and just enjoy the day."

I went to get my coat too. I loved playing in the snow. There are some things you're never too old to enjoy.

A Pint Please

We laughed and joked in the garden for hours. Everyone helped to build a huge snowman with a carrot for a nose, dark stones for eyes, and Jen even put a hat and scarf on the tubby fella.

We had snowball fights and Jen even convinced a very reluctant Peth to join in. She got into the swing of things eventually, and once in the zone she was a good shot —it bloody hurt when her oversized, compacted snowballs hit you in the head. I think she singled me out, like always.

When our fingers and toes were numb, and our noses as orange as the snowman's, we all headed inside for hot chocolate, marshmallows, and chocolate biscuits. Then we settled around a roaring fire in the living room and played cards while Woofer snored in the prime spot in front of the stove and chased after balls in his sleep.

After dinner, it was more cards, then we just hung out, chatting a little, but mostly everyone was lost to their own thoughts. By eight, Jen was zonked out and curled up on the sofa. Phage woke her up and she said a sleepy goodnight then they headed upstairs. Minutes later, Phage returned and said Jen was in bed and already asleep again.

"She's had a busy few days. Bet she'll sleep like a rock tonight," I said.

"After all the whispers, and the stress to her body, and all that excitement today, she's going to want to stay in bed all day tomorrow," agreed Phage.

"Don't forget, we have to go in the morning. It's gonna be a right pain with all this snow. The gritting trucks are about, even on the lanes, so it must be bad, but there's no way we can ride our bikes. Ugh, you know what that means?" I shuddered at the thought.

"It means Bernard," said Phage, grinning at my discomfort.

"Yeah. Nightmare. He's such a damn moaner. Always complaining about one thing or another. Oh, shit, we didn't let Tyr out either. Well, guess we should. And how about a pint afterwards?" Phage nodded eagerly. "Peth, you going to join us in the Necropub for a beer? Or maybe a glass of wine? I'll light the stove now, so once I've exercised Tyr and let Woofer out, it'll be nice and toasty in there too."

"As you wish." Peth nodded almost imperceptibly.

"What's wrong, Mother?"

"Oh, nothing. I was just thinking back to when you were Jen's age. Did we do things like this together? It was so long ago, and there have been so many children, so many days, but I don't think so. It's been a lovely time. I want to thank you both. It's been delightful. I felt young again. Free. No whispers, no magic, no worrying about my sisters, no need to act a certain way, keep up appearances. Just play. Oh, to be a child again."

Phage and I exchanged a glance. In all the years I'd known Peth, she'd never said such kind words, never shown a weakness or a warm, caring side like this before. It was weird, and unnerving. I half-expected her to jump up and say, "Gotcha!" She didn't, she just looked to Phage with what almost seemed like hope in her strange eyes. They shone red from the firelight.

Phage tensed instantly; she'd had too much crap over the years to go all soft and sentimental just because Peth was feeling nostalgic. "No, Mother, we did not play in the snow. You never once threw a snowball, never built a snowman with me, never played a game, did anything children like doing. You trained me, taught me about the Necroverse, told of things I wouldn't dream of telling Jen, and you made me study books and listen to the old women for hours at a time every single day."

"I'm sorry," Peth whispered. "I think I forget that children are so very different to us. That they need fun, to be carefree. Can you forgive me?"

"I don't know, but today was a good start. Mother, you've been gone so long, you missed so much of Jen when she was a little girl. It's only these last few years you've taken an interest. And we both know why that is. Because she's old enough now for you to start teaching her your ways. Your ways, not mine. Not ours. She is not one of your sisters. She is our daughter. Understand?"

"I do. I see such potential in her. She's so unique. No other has ever had what she undoubtedly will. And the dragon. The young unicorn. She will be unlike any Necro that came before her."

"That's what we're worried about, Peth," I told her. "We worry sick about her future. We see it too, of course we do. We know she's different. That's why we've tried to keep this madness from her. At least, the best we can. She mustn't know too much too early. There is plenty of time for her to develop, and she must do it at her own pace. No forcing things, no damn whisper training. And if you ever encourage her to go into the dark places I know you go, reach out and contact the sleeping giants out there in the Necroverse with all their power and their danger, then that will be the end of your relationship."

"I understand. But watch your tone. Don't forget who you are speaking to."

"I'm speaking to the grandmother of our daughter. Not a witch, not a powerful sister, not a strong whisperer. I'm talking to you, Pethach. My daughter's grandmother. Who she trusts, adores, and will follow if led."

Peth nodded her understanding. It was time I went to visit Tyr. I hadn't seen him since this morning, and he was asleep then. I was about to call Woofer, but he was whimpering, his legs moving like he was running, so he must still be chasing after balls. I left him by the fire and got out of the room. It was icy in there, despite the heat.

"Time to stretch your wings," I told Tyr as I opened the barn door and peered into the gloom.

"Tyr sleepy. And cold. Tyr not like cold. Want heat. Like summer."

"Yeah, well, I'm afraid you're out of luck, buddy. It's winter and the weather's extreme. You need to eat, that'll warm you up. Stoke the fire inside. You want to come out? Go hunt? It's dark, and there will be rabbits. You'll spot them a mile off against the snow."

"Tyr is hungry. Always hungry." The dragon stretched his long, tightly muscled body and craned his thick neck forward to study me. His orange and purple eyes glinted wickedly. Such knowledge and power hidden behind those juvenile orbs. So much potential. I wondered what the world looked like for him. How differently he saw things.

"Come on then, let's get you outside."

I stepped away from the doorway and Tyr spread his leathery wings. They rustled like old paper scratching across sand, a rasping, powerful sound. Small spikes, almost like extra claws, were now beginning to show at each segment of the wings—soon they'd be strong enough to kill with a swipe.

With a final stretch, he walked forward, head low, wings tucked back in so he could get through the door. As he emerged into the cold, his entire body rippled from head to toe. Poor guy hated this weather. Tyr readied himself then vanished as we'd told him to, so nobody would see him and no angry mob would descend.

I followed his progress for a while, able to spot him because of the gap in the snow, then he was gone.

"Enjoy the hunt, my friend. But no sheep or cows. Wild animals only," I reminded him.

"Tyr knows," he called back mentally, already scouring the land for his supper.

While he exercised, I headed to the Necropub. Snow was thick on the tin roof, and I had to scoop away a drift from the rotting door, then I yanked it open and was greeted with a familiar, joyous assault on my olfactory senses. Stale beer molecules and a hint of otherworldliness dashed out the exit, pleased to disperse in the frigid night air. I flipped the light on then closed the door behind me and smiled as I walked across the dirty floorboards and got the fire going in an ancient stove.

Within minutes the place was toasty. I eyed the three beer pumps greedily, but figured it was best to go get the others first before I settled in for a while.

I could have happily stayed alone though. When Peth and Phage got into one of their "discussions", the mood turned more frosty than the troll's head. With a sigh, I left the comfort and silence to tell them it was beer time. Then I remembered phones, and that I could stay put. It felt wrong, the epitome of lazy, but I was warm, and they might be arguing, so I called Phage instead and she sounded very eager to come join me.

Several minutes of impatient foot-tapping later, the door opened and cool air rushed in along with two very unhappy looking women.

"Hello ladies," I roared happily, feeling all warm and glowing from the fire that may have been running rather hot. "Hey Woofer. Get yourself comfortable. It's warmer in here than the house," I told him. He immediately went to his bed and curled up. Poor guy was done for.

"Hey," said Phage wearily.

Peth nodded a dour greeting and the two women stood there, looking sour and uncomfortable in each other's presence.

I sighed, and then I did something I swore I would never do. I encouraged them to get along. "Look, I know this isn't my place, and you'll both hate me for saying it, and I already hate myself, but we're family, right? Whatever you two have been bickering about—"

"We weren't bickering," snapped Phage.

"It doesn't matter. Because you're mother and daughter and you love each other. You disagree, hell, I disagree with just about everything Peth has ever said or done, but she's your mum and Jen's old granny." Damn, I was pushing it here. Peth sucked the warmth right out of the air with the look she gave me. "So here's an idea. Let's have a drink, forget this crappy day full of dead next-door neighbors, and—"

"Mrs. O'Donnell's dead?" gasped Phage.

"Um, no, let me rephrase that. Dead trespassers because really she's an ancient Necro and had us all fooled, even Peth."

"She didn't fool me. I knew. I just didn't say anything as it wasn't my place."

"Another thing you kept from me," hissed Phage. If looks could kill, Peth would be roasting in Hell and her daughter would be stomping on her grave.

"I do what I believe is right." Peth shrugged.

"Ooh, it's getting frosty in here, haha." Oops, that was about the worst thing to say. I wasn't very good at this. "Okay, look, I know I'm probably making this worse, but here's the deal. Peth, we trust you with our daughter, and that means a lot. Phage, we are going tomorrow. You need to make peace. And besides," I said conspiratorially, "we can't let *him* think we aren't getting along. You know what will happen then."

"Who's him?" asked Peth, puzzled.

"You know, *him*." I pointed down.

"Dwarves? The Devil? Worms? What are you talking about, boy?"

The air turned from cool to a veritable freezer.

"Okay, you know what? Fuck you, Peth. Fuck you, and fuck you again. I was trying to be a good son-in-law, but you just can't do it, can you? You can't be nice for one goddamn minute. You know what, just go. Fuck off back to your sisters and we'll figure something out."

"Soph," interrupted Phage.

"No, I've had it." I turned to Peth. "Don't call me 'boy' ever again. You condescending bitch. And don't pretend you didn't mean it as an insult. I tell you we're all family, and should make the effort, and you throw it back in my face. I've had it with you. Go on. Out!"

Woofer whined from his bed underneath the dartboard.

"I'm sorry." Peth actually hung her head a whole fraction of an inch. She kept her eyes on me, and she genuinely looked like she meant it. "I'm not used to this. To family. I know I was a terrible mother. We just had the whole sorry conversation about how I neglected my daughter, never made you feel welcome, failed in my duties as a Grandmother, and didn't show Phage the love she deserved. But I do love her. I love you all. I just cannot show it. I am from a different age. I never had affection, never knew how to give it. Today, being with you, playing cards, throwing snowballs, it made me ashamed. I am ashamed to be so distant, so cold, to not tell you how much I love you all. Yes, Soph. Even you. Will you forgive me? Both of you? Can we try again? I want to, if it isn't too late."

Phage ran to her mother and hugged her tightly. All she ever wanted was for her mum to say she loved her, show affection without an agenda. I let them have their moment, then moved in and kind of patted Peth on the shoulder before stepping back, feeling awkward.

I could kill a guy without thinking, but when it came to mothers-in-law, well, it absolutely terrified me.

"Now, how about that drink? And who were you talking about? Down there?" asked Peth.

"The Brewer," came a voice that sucked the life out of the world, turned your smile upside down, and yet made the most interesting of beers. You either loved it, and had a great time, or shit ran down your legs, you tripped your nuts off, and vowed never to drink again.

Guess what kind of night we had?

Trippy McNut-Nuts

At some point in the evening, we found ourselves pressing our backs to the door of the Necropub and sucking in greedily the sharp, crisp air of the outside world. It had been a hair-raising hour of beer drinking, head-splitting conversation with the Brewer, and plenty of glares between the two women.

We escaped the minute we were able, and not a moment too soon. After two pints each of a very peculiar concoction made by the resident Necroweird, we were all beginning to feel somewhat strange.

"Does it always make you excited like this?" asked Peth, eyes dancing with mirth. "Hehe, shall we dance?" Peth grabbed my hands and swung me around several times, then let me go—which meant flinging me at the nearest pile of snow—and raced around the crunchy land, skipping and giggling and generally acting about as out-of-character as you could get.

"He's such a lovely man," said Phage dreamily, as she stumbled off after her mother and they played a game of tag. They slipped and wrestled, whooped and laughed uproariously, and then they both lay down and made snow angels while I stood there, dazed, confused, discombobulated—I believed I was a fine gentleman named Harry for several minutes—and then the beer began to really take hold.

What had the resident drinks wizard said about this particular potion? That it was a family beer? He definitely said a "family" beer, complete with air quotes. The Brewer had grinned his special grin as he said it, then poured three froth-headed pints and slid them across the bar, watching eagerly as we sipped the amber gold and nodded our approval. He beamed with satisfaction and spent the next hour helping us down the liquid by placing his misshapen fingers at the bottom of the glass and tilting it. He really wanted us to drink this new brew.

The relief of escaping his presence mingled with the tingles that were creeping up my body from my toes— although I did have to check they were still there. All warm and fuzzy like puppies licking my ankles. The heat spread, and soon I was cocooned in a haze of beer-induced mind-fuckery as I began to absolutely trip my nuts off. Think a hundred magic mushrooms swilled down with an acid tab and several joints of pharmaceutical grade marijuana and you'd be getting close to the power of this particular beverage.

As visions of guffawing, flying snowmen forced away my doubts, my anger, Peth in general, my fear for my family, my dread of the day to come, and my absolute terror for what awaited my daughter, I locked the door and told Woofer that he'd better go inside before everyone started acting funny.

But there was no Woofer. Ah, yes, that's right, he'd morphed the moment the one and only Brewer appeared. The lucky guy was probably curled up beside the fire in the living room, which sounded like a very good idea about now.

My stomach rumbled. At least I think it did. I felt like I was one huge belly, empty and craving fuel. My tummy spoke to me, told me, yes, he was empty and I'd better fill him up or he might pop, and did I really want a popped belly on my conscience?

"No, belly, I don't want that on my conscience. But what should I do?"

"Go get a takeaway," he told me. "You must. This is your quest, Soph. To get takeaway. Make haste, before I go *boom*."

Giggling, and knowing I could be quick, I ran up to the house, arms flapping like an excited chicken, while the women played in the snow. In the kitchen, I grabbed our takeaway containers and thermoses and did one of the most exciting things of my life. I readied myself, then morphed to a chip shop in town and found myself standing outside the establishment with a stack of containers and a dumb smile on my face.

The place was thankfully deserted, so I wandered in to be greeted by the warm, greasy air and the joyous smells of frying food.

"Hurry, Soph, before it's to late," insisted my tummy.

"Don't worry, I'm gonna order now."

"Sorry, love, what was that?" asked a slim woman behind the counter.

"Oh, just talking to my tummy," I told her.

"Yeah, okay. What you want?" she snapped, eyeing me suspiciously.

I ogled the warming counter, where slabs of battered fish and long sausages smiled back at me invitingly.

"Fish and chips three times, six long smiley sausages, three gravy, one of those furry things, and a pie. Oh, and a lemon. No, two lemons." I grinned at her and nodded excitedly; my tummy gurgled with anticipation.

"Right you are. You want drinks too?" She indicated my flasks as I handed over the reusable food containers everyone had to provide now if they wanted takeaway.

"Yes, surprise me. Hehe." I handed them over and she began fulfilling my order.

Once ready, although I wasn't sure she'd remembered the furry thing and I couldn't find it now anyway, I almost snapped out of my high when she told me the price. With a gulp, I nevertheless scanned my card and took possession of the grub.

I ran away tittering like a stereotypical shy Japanese schoolgirl, and once out of sight I morphed back home and shouted, "Guess what I've got?" and as the two snow angels who had somehow become snowmen ran up to me, praising me and tearing the takeaway from my hands, I realized I'd just morphed so pain engulfed me as I sank to my knees, chortling like the idiot I undoubtedly was.

After that, it was all a bit of a blur. I remember eating chips that were frozen solid, and playing a game with a lemon I am still unsure existed. I locked Tyr in, as even in my addled state I was mindful enough to do that, and then I curled up next to Woofer by the fire and stared at the flames.

When I came to my senses in the morning, I found myself with my arm around Peth, Phage snoring in my chair, and Mr. Wonderful staring at me with utter disgust.

"And you call yourself the higher species." He shook his head in dismay, then commenced to clean his balls in a most purposeful manner.

Peth woke up, we stared at each other for the longest time, then she said, "Not a word. Not a single bloody word." She took my limp arm and moved it from where it was draped in a place it should never be on your mother-in-law, and got unsteadily to her feet.

"Mum's the word," I said, then guffawed very loudly. I think I was still a little high.

Freezing Shit

"What you doing?" asked a rather flustered looking Phage as she walked unsteadily across the kitchen like the floor was wobbling. She hung on to the back of a chair and watched me, her mind clearly elsewhere.

"Nothing. What are you doing?"

"I'm wondering why on earth we thought letting the notorious Brewer experiment on us was a good idea. Hey, did I imagine it or did you get takeaway? Were there lemons?"

"I got takeaway. Not sure about the lemons." I gestured to the washing up, where the Tupperware was draining after I'd cleaned up. I'd broken the cardinal rule you learn once you're a proper adult—never leave the dishes until the morning. It's depressing as fuck and takes ages.

"It was nice. I think. Damn, how much did that set you back?"

"Too much. Too many credits. Or is it dollars now? I can't keep track."

"Credits, I think. Didn't they do that worldwide change recently? Haha, ugh, I don't know. I can't get my head to work. And I only went shopping yesterday. The numbers don't make sense any more."

"No, I remember, I saw it on TV in hospital. It's universal credits. The entire world has the same currency now. Same economy, so they say. But it's bullshit. Um, at least I think it is. Ugh, I wish they'd just pick something and stick to it."

"It's to get everyone equal. Same amount of food, same energy, sharing the fuel, all that stuff."

"Yeah, tell that to some poor sod in the middle of the desert with no crops, no water, and no way to get power. How does that work?"

"I have no idea. Now what on earth are you doing?"

"We have to go today, right? And I figured, well, I figured I'd..."

"Soph, you know you stopped talking then, right?"

"What? Did I?"

"Yes."

"Oh."

There was an awkward silence as Phage came up beside me then looked at my preparations. "Seriously? You're going to dehydrate Tyr's poo?"

"Hey, don't judge me! I figured we might need it. And I am not eating it fresh. Look, the internet said if you dry this lump of hard poo, it will become hard as crystals and will even grow like them. And it concentrates the power, makes it so much better. Then you can just break off little bits, put it in a drink, sprinkle on your food, whatever. It might help. This will be a hard one, I can feel it. Doesn't hurt to be prepared."

"Just don't expect me to eat it. You wally." Phage pecked me on the cheek then left to check on Jen.

"I am not a wally," I muttered. "I'm just planning ahead." I fiddled with the dehydrator, managed to get Tyr's tummy trinkets inside on the flimsy trays, then powered it up, aware it was taking valuable juice but sure it was worth a gamble.

While it did its thing for the next hour or two, I went and sorted out the animals and did my morning chores. Somehow, I even managed a halfway decent workout. I moved on auto-pilot, my head fuzzy, my guts churning, my dread building as I thought of what lay ahead and how tough it would be to get this done. Would working together make us freeze up? Neither one of us wanting to show the other our dark side? The depths to which we sank. Or would we be invincible? More than twice as deadly, and thrive off each other's power?

I knew it would be the former. I did not want Phage to see the man I became when consumed by bloodlust. I hated that side of myself, but I accepted him, knew he was as much a part of me as the loving father and doting husband. For without the ability to lose control, have zero fear, be utterly confident in my ability to kill and survive, then I would have been dead centuries ago.

But would our relationship ever be the same again once we saw the monsters that lurked inside each of us? I hoped so, but I wasn't looking forward to testing it out.

"Hey, honey, how's the leg?" I asked Jen as she entered the kitchen. I stood guiltily in front of the dehydrator and tried to act casual.

"It's great! Look, the cast's off and I feel totally fine."

"That's amazing. It doesn't hurt at all?"

"Nope. So, what's the plan for today? More snowmen? How about a walk with Woofer?"

"Woofer want walk. Play ball with Woofer?"

"Sure," laughed Jen. "We can play ball, can't we, Dad?"

"Actually, and please don't get cross, your mother and I have to go away. Grandma will look after you for a few days. It won't be for long."

"What!? You can't be serious? You've only been home for what, a day and a bit? I've hardly seen you." Jen was starting to tear up and it broke my heart. I folded my arms around her and she sniffled into my shirt.

"I'm sorry, and if there was a way to stay, we would. But we can't."

"This is to do with what happens every year, isn't it? It's always around your birthdays. You always go. But this is Mum's birthday, so why are you going? Is it something to do with notes? Dad, you have to tell me. I'm starting to get scared. You never both go. What if you don't come back?"

"We'll come back. I know this is unusual, and I don't expect you to understand, not yet. You have to trust us on this, okay? Honestly, we have to go. We don't want to, but we have to."

"Okay. I trust you. Um, Dad?"

"Yes, my little apple?" I took in the scent of my daughter, which I knew she found weird, but I didn't care. Perfume and deodorant, toothpaste and make-up. Porridge and milk. It was perfect.

"Why is there poo in the dehydrator? Haha, I knew it!" Jen stepped away, her eyes full of mirth, and she pointed a finger at me, accusingly. "You read the Necronet, didn't you? You read about dragon poo and now you're drying it and going to eat it. Men!"

"Hey, whoa there, cowgirl. I am a grown man. I am over three centuries older than you. I know what I'm doing, you don't. I have experience, you don't."

"You have told a big lie. I haven't," countered Jen with a wicked grin. She loved getting one over on her old dad.

"Touché!" I ruffled her hair and she batted at my hands. I knew that would wind her up. "But listen, I don't want you eating it. We need to find out more about it. And I don't want you on the Necronet," I added hurriedly. "That's out-of-bounds until you're a hundred."

"Dad!"

"Okay, maybe ninety." I mussed her hair again then cuddled her tight. She squirmed, but I wouldn't let her go.

"What's all this? Cuddles without me?" asked Phage, looking divine in a tight purple turtleneck, black jeans, and a touch of dark stuff around her eyes. I wasn't sure what it was, as make-up had gone through so many changes because of packaging laws it could have well been ash from the fire or an expensive stick from a shop with some goop rubbed on it. Either way, she looked hot.

"You look hot," I told her.

"Ugh, so gross. Get a room," said Jen.

"And what do you know about getting a room?" I asked my daughter, who absolutely would never know what it meant.

Jen blushed and mumbled something, but I didn't push it.

"I told Jen we have to go. I explained we won't be long and not to worry."

"But he won't tell me why, Mum. Why are you going away? Dad's not recovered properly. Look at his face."

"What's wrong with my face?" I rubbed at my stubble and ran fingers through my hair.

"It's all tired looking. You've got bags under your eyes and you need your rest. You keep falling asleep in the chair."

"That's different. That's just resting my eyes."

"It's called sleeping, Dad. Everyone knows that. When you snore, you're asleep."

"Okay, but we have to go, regardless. Be good for Peth, do not let her lead you astray," I warned. "No Necronet, no poo, no snooping. Just walk Woofer and do your chores. You need to get the eggs, check the feed and water for the animals, and make sure you don't let the pipes freeze."

"Yeah, yeah. Should I wrap myself in cotton wool as well?"

"It would help," I said. "Maybe get Peth to Duct tape your bedding around you. Then I'd rest easy."

"Men!" sighed Jen.

"Men," agreed Phage.

"Men," I confirmed.

Then it was action stations. Jen went about her weekend chores, we got our gear together—there was more than usual because of the weather—and then it was time to go.

"You should have brought Kayin instead," said Jen, shivering as we stood outside the gate on the snow-covered gravel.

"She hasn't been far yet," said Phage. "And she's very young. But you should start riding her more now she's growing."

"I ride her almost every day. She's so fast, you wouldn't believe it. Nearly as fast as you, Bernard."

"Oh, great. I'm so happy for you both."

"What's up, big guy?" I asked, winking at Jen.

"Nothing. I love going on a long trip when it's snowing, rather than staying in my nice warm home with my family where there's plenty of food and maybe a little treat."

"Thought you'd sworn off the molasses? Remember what happened last time?" I'd told Jen what he'd done, so she giggled.

"That was an accident. And besides, Kayin did say she wanted to go."

"Blah, blah, blah. Better luck next time. You're coming, as we need you. A team, remember?"

"I remember," he sulked. "But how come I have to do all the work?"

"Because you love us so much."

Jen giggled and turned to Phage. "Don't worry, Mum. Bernard's happy to help out."

"Good. Right, time to go. Mother, look after Jen. Jen, look after Mother."

"We'll be fine," said Peth, who had been very quiet this morning. "Be safe."

"Always."

"Bye, honey. Don't forget, no misbehaving." I kissed the top of Jen's head, then wrapped my arms around her. "Look after yourself," I whispered. "Love you."

"Love you too," she whispered back.

I nodded to Peth, Phage cuddled Jen and gave her mother a perfunctory hug, and then we got into the cart. Bernard trotted along the track, turned onto the lane, and we were alone.

A Strange Beginning

"Well, this is weird," I told Phage after we'd been going for ten minutes in almost total silence.

"Haha, isn't it? I thought it was just me. I can't get my head in the right place."

"Me neither. This is the time you question everything, thoughts go around and around, you wonder yet again what the point of Necronotes is, what it all means, if they're watching your every move, if there are aliens somewhere tuning in to the action, and cursing yourself for the bad things you've done and questioning if you deserve the happy life you have at home. Um, or is that just me?"

"Oh, thank god! I'm so glad you said that. It's exactly how I feel. Always thinking I don't deserve to be happy, despising myself for the things I've done, the lives I've taken. I hate this, Soph. I hate it more than anything. But I know I won't stop. I know I will kill and keep on killing if it means I can live. Is that wrong?"

"I think it's the only choice we have. We do what we have to and we live with the consequences. We've got to get it together this time, though. I don't want to be unable to perform because you're watching. Ugh, that sounds weird."

"You've never had a problem performing before," she said with a twinkle in her eye.

"No, but my wife wasn't stabbing some stranger in the eye the other times."

"I do like a knife," she said. "Ugh, sorry. Gosh, we truly are terrible people."

"Maybe."

Silence descended once more. It felt like we were strangers. Unable to tell each other the things we wanted to say the most.

"Hey, I know what will cheer us up."

"What?" asked Phage, a little too quickly.

"Damn, it's like we're on a first date."

"I know, right? So weird. Come on, what will cheer us up?"

"Wait and see," I told her with a smile.

"This is it? Your idea of a cool thing to lighten the mood? Necrosmoke?"

"What's wrong with that?"

"I don't smoke," pouted Phage.

"Ah, but I do. And besides, we can have a gossip with Pam. I haven't seen her since the attack, but you have. Come on, it'll be fun. You could even try the new gadgets. The twatcigs."

"Ecigs," she corrected.

"I think you'll find I was right. They've got melon," I taunted.

"What's wrong with your eyebrows?"

"I was wiggling them. You know, in a mysterious way. Like wizards do."

"Trust me, that was not mysterious. You're no wizard. You're many things, but no wizard. Okay, come on, let's go see Pam."

"And the best thing is, she said I could have free tobacco for the rest of my life."

"Aha," said Phage as I helped her off the cart like a gentleman, "but I think she meant once a year, and this isn't really your turn, is it?"

"Damn, hadn't thought of that," I said glumly as I pushed open the door. The bell rang, then I let Phage enter first.

"Pam, are you there?" I called jovially, then frowned at all the stupid, neatly aligned bottles of mysterious liquid sitting like idle soldiers on glass shelves.

"Where?" she asked, appearing from out back looking like an angel with big boobs, because that's exactly what she was.

"Huh?"

"It was a joke," said Pam. She flicked a plait over her shoulder and smiled at Phage. "Hey Phage. This is an unexpected visit. You've never been here before, have you?"

"No, but I've heard plenty. He practically drools when he talks about it."

"And that's because of the tobacco, not because of Pam," I added, knowing as I spoke it was an idiot move and I was digging a hole I had until now not been standing in.

"Men are so stupid," muttered Pam.

"Thats right, haha. Not our fault. It's genetic. And um, what was a joke?"

"Forget it. Anyway, what's cookin'?"

"I wanted to cheer Phage up, so I brought her here."

"Like I said, stupid," said Pam, giving Phage a sympathy smile.

"How are you doing?" I asked her. "All recovered?"

"Yes, I'm fine, and thank you. Glad you're finally out of the hospital. That was a rough few months. You doing okay too?"

"Fine. A few twinges, but I'm good. Have to be. We got a thing to do together."

"A thing?" Pam mulled it over then her eyes widened. "Shit. That's unlucky."

"Sure is. Now, what have you got for me? Something fat and juicy and stinky, I hope." Both women just stared at me. "What?"

"Like I said, tobacco is on the house. Although, haven't you still got some left from last time? It was only a few months ago. Thought your smoking was a once-a-year thing."

"So did I," said Phage.

"Hey, I've been stressed."

"Haven't we all?" nodded Pam. She nonetheless sorted me out with a nice bumper pack of dark tobacco, all neatly tied with a piece of string.

We hung around longer than I usually would, chatting, talking about the weather and asking after business, that sort of thing, but soon enough it was time to leave.

With a wave, and my lungs already burning with anticipation, we moved from the warmth into weather as un-British as a long hot summer used to be.

Wind blew fresh snow into our faces, already drifting against the buildings, and we reluctantly hopped back onto the cart. Bernard trotted morosely past tightly huddled houses and places of business. The whole scene was like something out of a Christmas card—timber framed Tudor buildings with snow on the roofs, even a few illegal fires burning, so smoke blew at right angles from weathered chimney stacks. If our minds hadn't been so grim, it would have been an enjoyable sight.

We left Shrewsbury and headed north into the unknown.

I shouldn't have been surprised, but Phage was an expert at traveling during inclement weather. I'd believed I had it bad traveling during the summer when the heat sapped all strength and you could never drink enough water. Traveling during a blizzard was a whole different ball game.

It was a struggle to stay warm, your energy drained so fast as you tried to stop freezing to death, and our thermos of tea lasted until ten minutes outside of town then was gone. But Phage sorted everything. She knew where to stop to get hot water refills from friendly small businesses, had several places to rest that were sheltered but private, and had winter gear stowed in the back of the cart I would never have thought of bringing.

But we'd still only just begun our journey, had been traveling away from Shrewsbury for a matter of hours, and we had a long, long way to go. Our destination wasn't particularly far as the dragon flies, but having to stick to main roads and avoid the lanes both of us favored meant we would travel far out of our way to circle around and back down to the location deep in the heart of West Wales.

Welsh roads were crap at the best of times, there being no real motorways away from the southern route that led from Bristol in England to the capital of Wales, Cardiff. Apart from that, it was all windy roads and the old bypasses, built when we had to worry about traffic volumes polluting small towns and villages. Now they were empty, and especially so on a day like this when the only people out on horseback, or in carts and carriages, were the insane, the desperate, or the Necro.

Swaddled under thick coats, woolen hats, gloves so thick it was hard to tell if your fingers were still there, and with blankets wrapped over our shoulders, we huddled close together and let Bernard move at his own speed. We were alone in a world of nothing. Everything was white, but it was impossible to see much of anything as the wind howled and the snow flurries sped past, stinging what little of my face was exposed. We could have been anywhere, we could have been nowhere at all.

The only constant was Bernard's moaning. Phage sure got off lightly being deaf to his endless, boring complaining. Like he was the only one out here.

In the end, even that stopped, as he said his mind was so numbed by the cold that his brain was too sluggish to form a coherent thought and transmit it to me. I knew he was lying, but I was used to it. If it kept him quiet, that was fine by me.

After hours and hours of not getting much of anywhere at all, Phage told Bernard to take a turn and we headed down a shallow incline then through a modest village I'd never visited before.

There was nobody about, no shops were open, no lights shone. It was like the end of the world. Armageddon, but death by snowman instead of nuclear meltdown and blinding fire bombs.

"On your right, Bernard," directed Phage. "You remember, don't you?"

"Does she expect me to answer?" Bernard asked me.

"Do what you would if I wasn't here," I told him.

"What was that?" asked Phage.

"Just talking to Bernard."

"What did he say?"

"He said you look lovely today, like a model."

"Aw, that's sweet." Phage smiled; her cheeks were very rosy.

Bernard dutifully headed down a wide cutout between houses, then under an arch. We found ourselves in a cobbled courtyard where the snow had been cleared and a narrow stable block was built along a high brick wall as a lean-to shelter for grumpy unicorns or sweet-natured horses. The place was deserted.

With Phage hushing my questions, we unhitched Bernard, relieved him of his covering of snow, then all moved into a large, dry stall. We patted down the grump and shook out our coats, the warmth and shelter welcome. Within minutes, our fingers and toes tingled as they thawed. I breathed deeply of the straw and old animal smell that had soaked into the fabric of the building over years.

"How are you feeling now, Bernard?" asked Phage kindly.

Bernard whinnied and nodded his head several times. I guess they had their own way of communicating. Phage pecked him on the nose and told him he was a great help. Bernard batted his huge long eyelashes and nuzzled under her chin.

"What the hell, Bernard? When I'm with you all I get is grief and a kick up the arse!"

"You don't treat me like Phage does. And besides, she can't hear me."

"Bernard's such a sweetie," cooed Phage, rubbing his head and staring at him all doe-like.

"Yeah, real angel."

"Come on. We'll see you later, Bernard." Phage dragged me out into the snow then across the courtyard and through a weathered door set into a traditional flint and brick wall on the back of a tall house. Inside was like a sauna after the freezing exterior.

"What is this place?" I asked my grinning wife, as she pulled off her coat and shook out her hair.

"You'll find out."

"Is it even open? Is it a pub? A cafe? What?"

"Of course it's open. We're inside. Come on." Phage offered her hand and I took it. Her fingers were pink, same as mine, the heat slowly returning circulation.

We moved down a narrow, dark corridor, with a wooden floor and black painted walls and ceiling. Ahead, strange lights strobed. I could hear music. Johnny Cash, if I wasn't mistaken. Ring of Fire, which was either apt, or the opposite, I couldn't decide which.

We burst from darkness into otherworldly light. A room painted as black as the corridor was strung with fairy lights, LED strips of the most modern kind, that apparently used no electricity and worked off the heat of other appliances, even ambient heat if the room was warm enough, and several other strange light sources of mostly purples and blues. It didn't feel cold though, it felt warm and inviting.

"What is that smell? Have I died and actually made it to heaven? Is that it? You really are an angel?" I breathed in deeply through my nose and felt the tang of herbs and spices, garlic and chili, hit the back of my throat.

"That, my friend, is the smell of the best curry this side of Birmingham," said a tall, thin Indian man as he put a strong hand on my shoulder and beamed at me.

"It sure smells like it. But that's a tall boast. You know Birmingham has some of the best curry houses outside of India."

"And I have been to every one of them over the many years I have been alive. Trust me, you are in for a treat."

Phage smiled sweetly at me then the man. "Soph, this is Aakesh. Aakesh, this is Soph, my husband."

"So good to see you again, Phage. And Soph, so nice to meet you at last. Your reputation precedes you, I am afraid. I have heard many stories of you over the years."

"Nothing good, I expect."

"Oh, haha, Phage said you were a kidder. No, nothing good, but when is it ever good when it's tales of death and derring-do whilst in mortal danger? Such is the life of a Necro. But you are alive, and so am I, so that counts for something in this world. It is a thing to be celebrated, to be proud of. Come, be seated, sit by the fire. You picked a bad day to be out, but we must do what we must do. Please, over here." Without us having much choice, Aakesh led us to a table for two close to a roaring open fire in a massive nook. Flames crackled and large logs burned brightly. Shiny cutlery and spotless glasses glinted orange from the reflected flame.

"Now, is there anything in particular, or shall I just bring you what's best? Yes, I shall bring you a feast." He smiled, then bowed and dashed off.

"He's a talker," I noted.

"He is," nodded Phage. "But he's very proud of this place, and he produces the most amazing food."

"He's the chef?"

"In a way. He's the waiter. Front of house. Everything. I come here every year."

"You never said. How come?" I pulled off my coat, then my sweater. I was boiling already.

"I guess because we don't talk about what we do every year, I didn't want to. Too close to home sometimes. All part of the same thing."

"Makes sense. Well, thanks for bringing me. I'm amazed it's open."

"Aakesh opens every single day of the year, no matter what. People are always passing through and he likes to always be here for them. Offer a friendly face, a smile either on the way to fulfill a note, or when you really need it on your return. It's his calling, at least that's what he says. His destiny. Of the curried kind."

"That's kind of him."

"Oh, and he charges a fortune."

"You look beautiful by the firelight," I told my lovely wife. "Glowing and fresh."

"Why, thank you, handsome man."

"Here is your food! It is so sweet to see two people so much in love together. We don't get many couples. It warms my heart." Aakesh unloaded a huge tray piled with enough food to feed a small army.

"That smells absolutely amazing. Wow. Look at it all. How'd you get the spices these days? I thought it was impossible." I was genuinely interested, as ever since the embargoes and trade agreements, you pretty much ate what your country produced unless you were somewhere where the terrain and climate made food production nigh on impossible.

Aakesh frowned, confused.

"Oh, I haven't told him," giggled Phage.

Aakesh grinned. "Then that explains it. My dear friend, I do not cook here. I am Aakesh, Lord of the Sky. When a valued customer places an order, I morph back to my home village where my dear mother and father prepare the food. This is real Indian food, direct from India. Made the old way, the same as it has been done for many centuries. Nothing else compares. Eat. Enjoy. There is plenty more if you wish it." With a bow and a flourish, he left.

"Now I understand why it's so expensive. It's not the food cost, it's the air miles."

Phage laughed. "He's amazing at morphing. He's dedicated his whole life to it. He says it still hurts, but he's practiced yoga for centuries so he disassociates from the pain and he's done the same trip so many times now that it's like second nature."

"That really is impressive. But Peth said nobody could morph that far. I thought I'd pretty much beaten the record."

"Mother doesn't know everything. But yes, Aakesh is very unusual. A true one-off. Soph, the distance you morphed is extraordinary. None of the other witches had ever gone as far so quickly, but there are exceptions to every rule."

"Of course. Now, let's see if the hype is as good as you both say." I was salivating like Bernard confronted with a bucket of molasses.

We tucked in, and spent an incredible hour eating the best food I had ever tasted in my life. And trust me, I've been around.

"Would you care for anything else?" asked Aakesh, appearing like a wraith from nowhere.

"I couldn't eat another thing. I am absolutely stuffed."

"Me too," said Phage with a groan and a smile.

"Then let me thank you for visiting. You are welcome to stay as long as you wish. There is a bed upstairs. One of only one guest room, haha. It is free this evening. Not free, as in no cost, but a trifle compared to the meal. I have changed the sheets. It is a nice room, Phage, is it not?"

"It's lovely, Aakesh, but I don't know if we should. We do need to get on."

"Nonsense. It is almost dark already. In half an hour it will be black outside. Stay, get an early start. I can make breakfast," he taunted, in a sing-song voice.

We smiled as we exchanged a glance. Should we?

"Let's do it!" we blurted at the same time.

So we did. And it was awesome. And I slept like a baby. I don't believe I had ever slept twelve straight hours in my life, but that night, full of Aakesh's amazing food, with a compact stove heating the room, and my wife curled up beside me, I had the best damn sleep of my life. So did Phage. We awoke in the morning cuddled up close, then started off the day in the best way possible.

No, not that. We had Indian breakfast. Real Indian breakfast.

And we also fooled around. Must have been the spices.

Ho, Ho, Ho

Wrapped up, toasty and relaxed from the blazing fire in Aakesh's awesome restaurant, we said our goodbyes regrettably, then held hands as we left the strange glow of the blue room and entered the dark solemnity of the black hallway.

At the door, we turned to each other and smiled, then sighed and switched into Necro mode.

The fun and games were over. It was time to get gnarly as our cocoon of pleasure was about to be popped. I felt like we'd been on honeymoon, somewhere safe, isolated, alone in the world where I could imagine everything was normal. All that was about to change. Time to go kill. Time to break the spell.

I released Phage's hand and pulled on the door. We were confronted with a wall of snow. We stared at each other then burst out laughing. Like what we were doing wasn't mad enough already, now this?

"It's definitely back down to earth with a bump," I told Phage.

"I wonder what it's like out there? Can we stay here?" she asked, smiling.

"I wish. Come on, Bernard is going to be so miserable."

"Poor thing, he'll be freezing."

"Don't let him fool you. I get his moaning all the time. Too hot, too cold, too this, too that. It's a lie. He's a unicorn. He can't feel the cold, or get too hot. He likes it cool, sure, but he remains a constant temperature no matter what. I think you could probably chuck him in a fire and he wouldn't know the difference. He just likes to complain."

"But you said he likes it cool. You've always said that."

"I know. He does. But he doesn't actually feel it. That's unicorns for you. Annoying."

"Still, he might be cold." Phage chuckled rather manically, then shook her head. "Sorry, just feeling strange. It's been so nice, hasn't it? When did we last ever come out alone?"

"Before Jen was born. A long time ago. It's been an absolute delight. Let's do it again soon."

"Yes, let's. Soph, we will be okay, won't we?"

I took my wife's hands and stared into her eyes. "We will be fine. We will do this. We can do this. We will do what we have to and get home to our daughter. Together. Now, let's go get our unicorn."

We pushed on the snow and the top few feet collapsed out into the courtyard, revealing a winter wonderland.

All was white, and still. Snow fell gently, all possible sound muted by the thick blanket that vanquished the world as you know it. Heavy snowfall is such a strange thing. You get used to the world looking a certain way and then suddenly it's completely changed. Nothing is familiar, everything is alien. Everything transforms. It's a new world. A strange, white, quiet one. I felt like I'd morphed to the North Pole.

The world was washed clean, covered over, ready to begin again. It was like the end of days, or the beginning of a new era.

We shoved at the snowdrift still up to our chest, and then were forced to scoop the snow away. In the end, the only solution was to take a running jump and leap out into the white world beyond. Laughing, and feeling like kids again, we scrambled about until finally we were free and standing almost knee deep in thick, fresh snow. We waded over to find Bernard and there he was, snoring away in his stall, the room warm from his body heat.

"Time to wake up, Bernard," said Phage as she patted his flanks.

A lazy eye opened and our ride out of here was immediately ready to moan. "You took your time. It's freezing in here."

"He says he's freezing," I told Phage.

"It's boiling hot. Like a sauna," she laughed. "You've had a lovely sleep, haven't you?"

"I may have dropped off for a few minutes, but I was awake all night, shivering."

"Yeah, yeah, come on, time to get up and leave. We have a lot of ground to cover today and it's going to be slow going."

Bernard made a big deal of standing, like he was too exhausted, then peered out of the door at the deep snow. "I can't go out in that. Look at it. Oh well, guess we're stuck," he said, not sounding glum at all.

"No way. We're going. Come on, out you come. You might want to melt the snow a bit, or we'll never get out of the yard," I told him.

With a deep snort, and a lot of eye-rolling, Bernard nonetheless moved out of the stall, melting the snow as he went by the power of his own stupidity, which cleared a very large area indeed.

"Well done, Bernard," said Phage, encouragingly.

"I hate snow."

"And you hate heat, the rain, the wind, the sun, blah, blah, blah. Come on, let's get you hooked up. Damn, the cart's covered in snow. Look at it."

With a sigh, Phage and I spent the next ten minutes clearing it and sorting our gear out. Everything was solid from the freezing temperature, and by the time we'd finished we were wet, numb, and knackered.

Then more fumbling and cursing as we hitched Bernard up to the cart and got ourselves comfortable.

Phage took the reins as she still insisted I was rubbish at being in control, even though I was dealing with horses long before she was even born. I didn't argue, as it meant I could keep my hands in my jacket pockets.

"Okay, let's do this," I said, with all the positive vibes I could muster.

"Off we go, Bernard. Let's get back onto the main roads and then power up," said Phage. "The sooner we can get some momentum, the sooner we'll arrive. There shouldn't be a soul around so we should make good time."

Famous last words.

It took us half an hour just to get out of the village. The snow was deep on the small road and the cart repeatedly got stuck. Bernard refused to help. He moved as slowly as possible, giving us no momentum, and I'm sure he headed for the deepest drifts on purpose. But we got out of there, and took a turn onto the main road which was relatively clear thanks to the grit that had been laid down to stop the country coming to a complete standstill.

Bernard walked sedately through the wet mush as we headed north. Several vehicles and huge, multi-axled trucks pulling half a dozen trailers trundled past, not much faster than Bernard. The supply chain had to operate no matter what, so these huge behemoths were a regular sight nowadays.

"Those things are bloody massive. Bet the drivers are nice and toasty in their cabs."

"How do they turn? They can't get around bends with all those containers hitched on to them."

"They deliver just to the ubermarkets. They're all built to accommodate them. But the small stores are going to really struggle with this weather. You can bet their roads aren't cleared."

"I wish we could travel by car. I hardly got to do it before everything changed," said Phage wistfully.

"It's coming back, trust me. This has gone on too long now. People won't stand for it much more. There are loads more risking driving now. They don't care if they get locked up. At least that way they know they'll be fed and looked after. I bet the prisons are overrun."

"Nope, they aren't," said Phage smugly. "I heard a thing on the radio the other day. Apparently they're closing at least half as crime is so low. No driving, no crime. People can't travel so they aren't misbehaving. There's more petty crime, stealing from small shops and the like, but murder is at an all-time low, burglary too, as so many people are at home more. And with all the drones and cameras covering nearly the whole country, it's easier to get caught. Everyone's actually behaving."

"I guess there's not as much worth stealing, either. Well, that's great. But I still want a car. Imagine going on jobs when we can just drive there. It'll be weird."

"It'll be awesome." Phage huddled closer. I pulled the blanket tighter over our heads so we could keep the warmth in.

A ridiculous convoy of the beasts of the road idled past lazily, one after the other, the noise defeating. We were forced almost onto the verge where the snow was deeper and the going nonexistent. We waited it out while they passed, a strange reminder of what it took to keep a country running.

Eventually, the road was clear, and we wasted no time getting back onto the snow-free section and picking up speed.

The wind howled, bitter air bit at our exposed faces, Bernard moaned, and I wondered if we'd make it.

"Bernard, you have to push yourself," Phage told him. "We won't get there otherwise. Please go fast. I mean your special kind of fast."

"My head won't work properly. My brain's numb."

"The faster you go, the warmer you'll be," I said, playing along with his nonsense. "Come on, we can get there today if you do your thing. We'll find shelter then."

Bernard nodded glumly, and gradually his pace increased. And then we were off. Cocooned in his special glow of fuzziness. The world changed from bitter and uncaring to warm and inviting. Dreams of puppies and meadows filled my mind as Bernard rode a rainbow of his own making. We were in the air, Bernard's legs moving languidly, defying the speed at which we traveled.

We shot past the convoy and other unfortunates on horses or in carts because they had no choice but to travel, and then for miles and miles the road was empty. Just a blur of magical mayhem as Bernard rushed north, then we began to circle back around and finally it felt like we were getting somewhere.

Time lost meaning. We could have been traveling for hours or seconds. There was no real way of knowing. My head was fuzzier than a dwarf's chin. I couldn't hold a thought, just knew I had a dumb smile on my face and I was no longer cold. Phage had a faraway look in her eyes, and the same stupid smile.

We were in Bernard's realm now, a teaser of what was going on, or not, inside his head. Thoughts were like birds; they kept flying away. The world was less complicated, but the difference between ours and his was that we weren't miserable. We were feeding off his magical energy, and it was positive. Leaving him to soak up the glum and pound it over the head with a blunt object until it succumbed and promised to keep him grumpy and dumb.

Bernard moved faster and faster, higher and higher, until we were like Father Christmas, flying through the air on a magical sleigh, the snow whizzing past us as we careened around the world, not here to dish out presents but to take things, destroy them.

And then, just like that, with a sudden rush of dour thoughts, I snapped out of the loveliness and was brought back to reality with a cold, sharp shock.

"We're here," said Bernard glumly.

"Where? What do you mean?"

"I mean, we're here." Bernard turned and looked at me, putting all he had into a scornful glare, like I was the dumb one.

"He says we're here." I told Phage. "Phage? Hello?" I waved my hand in front of her face. She was staring off into the distance. I followed her line of sight and looked at the huge castle looming high on a hill like something out of a fantasy novel.

"He's right," she whispered.

"Bernard, how the fuck did you do that? You never go all the way at that speed. You always slow down, can never take sharp bends or get too close. I thought you had to build up to these things?"

"I do. I've been slowing for ten minutes, but it only took a couple of seconds to make the trip. I told you, I was about to turn blue. I wanted this done. Can we go home now?"

"No, we can't go home. We've only just arrived. We have to, you know, do what we came here for."

"Kill the people in the castle," he said. "Go on then. I'm hungry."

"He's hungry, and he wants to go home," I told Phage.

"Aren't we all? Well done, Bernard. I don't know how you did it, but you did. Is this really the place?" Phage removed her gloves and fumbled about with her phone until she brought up the Necroapp. She checked the location then looked at the castle again. She frowned.

"Is it where we should be?"

"No. It's a castle. But it's not *the* castle."

We both turned and stared at Bernard.

"You fucking dick," I told him.

"Utter twathorn," said Phage.

"What? It's a castle, isn't it?"

I sucked in a deep breath and counted to ten while we glared at Mr. Numpty. "Bernard," I said calmly, "castles are different. And located in different places. You can't just pick one that's closest and say we've arrived."

"That's just silly," agreed Phage.

"So, why the FUCK did you bring us here?" I screamed. Counting to ten never worked with Bernard. There wasn't a number high enough to keep your cool.

"I thought it would be funny?" he ventured.

"Did you? Did you though?" I asked, squinting my eyes to read his dumb, long face.

"Maybe?"

"You didn't, did you? You just forgot where to go, and figured we might not notice, right?"

"That is one possibility." Bernard had the good grace to lower his head and look abashed.

"So, do you know where we're actually going?"

"Could you remind me?"

I sighed. "Do you need to see the map, or can you read Phage's mind if she looks at her phone and follows the route with her eyes?"

"Of course I can!" he said, indignant.

"Can what? Read her mind, or see the map?"

"Um. Both?" he said optimistically.

"So you can read her mind and picture the route? Yes?" Sometimes it was like talking to a rock. A really dumb one.

"Yes."

"Then why didn't you?"

"I got confused. Must have taken a wrong turn, and I didn't want to slow down and have it seem like I didn't know where I was going."

"So you figured you'd chance it and see if we noticed?"

"Maybe."

"So dumb." I turned to Phage and explained.

She was not a happy camper. Neither was I. Like our stress levels weren't high enough already.

"Okay, let's try this again shall we?"

"If we must," grumbled Bernard.

"Yes, we must. Come on, help us out here. You know how much we hate this. And you're making it worse. Let's just get going. And please, pretty please, with fucking sprinkles on top, take us to the right place this time."

"You got it!"

Phage and I shook our heads at the sheer idiocy that confronted us, but she nevertheless studied the route slowly and carefully then showed it to Bernard, just to be on the safe side.

We took our places, again, and crossed our fingers as Bernard did about a hundred-point-turn as he wasn't good at reversing, then set off at an excruciatingly slow place.

Trying Again

It turned out we weren't as far away as I'd assumed. I'd imagined that Bernard-the-directionally-challenged had taken us in completely the wrong direction and possibly ventured into another country, but we were still in Wales, just a little north of where we needed to be.

As the miserable magical misfit meandered morosely through a snow-covered landscape, I vowed once more never to take him with me. It simply wasn't worth the hassle. I would have rather waded through waist-high snowdrifts than have the blood clot-inducing stress of dealing with his nonsense. Why couldn't my unicorn be smart? Kayin, who would be Jen's, was already ten times more intelligent than her mother and father combined, but at least with Betty she was sweet and cute with it. Bernard was just... Well, he was Bernard.

Yes, he had saved my life, and yes, he did a lot of cool stuff, but no, it wasn't enough. When I thought of all the windows I'd had to repair over the years, it made me shiver, and not from the cold.

"Why are you scrunching your face up like that?" I asked Phage.

"Mwf, proof, fog wet."

"You what?"

Phage relaxed her mouth and stopped her weird frown, then told me, "I'm trying to keep the route in my head. So Bernard doesn't have another accident."

"He does this a lot, doesn't he? Ha! I knew it! See, this is why I always prefer my bike."

"Some of us don't always have that luxury," she snapped. "You get to go in the summer. I travel when it's either raining, snowing, or just freezing cold. So I have to take him a lot of the time."

"Oh, right." That told me, and then some.

"I apologize. I didn't mean to snap. It's just beyond stressful."

"I know. It's okay. That's what I'm here for. To be shouted at and punched."

"No, I mean it. This isn't your fault. It's theirs. Soph, I want to go home."

"Me too. More than anything. Soon. We'll be home soon. Everything will be warm and cozy. The fire will be lit, Jen will be smiling, hopefully your mother will leave the moment we walk through the door, and everything will be perfect." I put my arm around her and beamed.

"It will, won't it? Just us. Our home. Together."

"Absolutely. A family."

Phage smiled again, but her eyes were downcast and they didn't twinkle. Then she resumed her face-pulling so Bernard wouldn't decide to just walk off a cliff. Hopefully.

Once we navigated the winding lane that led to the wrong castle, we emerged onto a wide main road. Bernard stopped, then began to turn left. Then he stopped, and swept right. Then he paused and turned his head to squint at Phage. We both saw the look she gave him and neither of us said a word. He simply faced front swiftly, and when Phage pulled on the rein in her right hand Bernard had the sense to follow her direction.

We were losing valuable time now, and no way did any of us want to get stuck in the middle of nowhere for the night, so Bernard began to increase his speed. But then he slowed to a sedate trot again.

"It's straight on this road for ten miles, then you take a left at the roundabout across the bypass, keep going for two miles, take a right, then follow the small road until we get there. Think you can manage that?" Phage hissed. "Or should I draw you a map and stick it to your stupid fucking face!?" she screamed.

Bernard acted sensibly for once, and didn't turn around.

"You guys really do have all the fun, don't you?" I chortled.

Phage glowered. "Do not speak to me," she hissed.

"Come on, it's okay. I've never seen you like this before."

"I know. Sorry Bernard. I'm not myself at all. I don't want to do this. I don't want us to be together when we kill people."

"Neither do I. But we can, and we must. We'll do this, and then we will all go home. The three of us. Phage, look at me."

She turned and smiled weakly. "You're so strong."

"I'm not. I just know nothing can stop us. You're awesome, I'm awesome, and Bernard is Bernard."

"I heard that."

"I know you did. Now hurry up, please. Can't you see this is upsetting Phage? No messing about. Get us there, and stay focused."

Soon we were wrapped in the dreams of a unicorn. It couldn't have come too soon. In all the years Phage and I had been together, I had never known her to lose it like this. Apart from the thing about the cheese. Curse this cheese shortage.

Smiling puppies and rain made of warm marshmallows soon wrapped us in lovely glowing visions as Bernard tore through the bleak Welsh landscape on his way to who knew where. I tried not to dwell on the fact that after all these years together, he had never once showed me that he could travel at such speeds without the usual slowing at various stages. He could have saved me a lot of heartache.

"We're here," said Bernard as he took a turn up a meandering track. The only signs of life were animal prints in the thick snow he kicked at as his breath clouded.

"Where?" I asked suspiciously.

"At the castle."

"Which one?"

"The right one."

"Good. Thanks. Phage, he says this is it. The right place this time."

"It looks like it. That's the picture on the phone. See." She showed me the picture but I didn't need it. I looked at the castle high up on the hill and knew this was the correct destination.

"Great. Yep, well done that unicorn. Okay, how about over into the trees so we can have shelter and stay hidden? But let's get a proper look first."

Bernard whinnied quietly then dragged us through the drifting snow as the wind picked up and loose ice kicked up from his hooves.

We found a suitable spot a few minutes later, nice and hidden, but with a view up to the castle if we broke cover.

Phage and I jumped down and moved off a ways to get our first impression of the place.

"We have to go inside and deal with whoever's there. Damn, this is nothing like anything I've done before. How do we know who it is? It could be full of people."

"On a day like this? I doubt it. It'll be empty. It would be empty even if it was a nice day in the summer. All these things are running on skeleton crews, have been for years now. Nobody comes. It's a crime what happened to the National Trust. All those amazing buildings, all those gardens. The visitors dried up because how many people will ride a horse to look at a castle? Not that anyone's allowed to travel anyway. It breaks my heart to think how many places have gone to ruin in the last decade."

"I wish I could have seen them all before it was too late," said Phage sadly.

"It's not too late. Lots of places still have volunteers to look after the gardens and buildings. It's not that bad. And hey, when this is all over and things return to normal, then we'll hit every castle in the country."

Phage grinned. "You have a deal. So how many people do you think will be at a big castle like this? It's beautiful."

"Today? My guess would be none. Maybe a tiny crew of volunteers. Or could be a family or someone alone lives here. But we aren't here for a visit. So who knows? Could be a gang of mental witches. A posse of pretenders, or a single person that our overlords needed both of us to defeat."

"That's depressing."

"Sure is."

"If you have both finished talking nonsense? Do you think you can get me out of this torture device and feed me?"

"Bernard's hungry. Coming, Bernard. Hey, out of interest, what would happen if you didn't eat? You know, what with you being immortal?" I winked at Phage. She smiled.

"I would be weak, and in a bad mood."

"So, no difference then?"

"Stop teasing him. Thank you for getting us here so fast, Bernard. That was amazing. Um, for a second attempt."

Bernard nodded his head and shook his mane in reply. It was great to have Phage back being polite and not screaming. Bernard seemed relieved too.

We moved away from the open and down the rise then into a dense forest. It was still, there was less snow, and it offered shelter and protection from anyone looking from the castle. We continued in until we were entirely hidden, then I began clearing an area for us to set up camp.

"It doesn't seem right to have arrived so quickly. Even with the hiccup. I mean, where's the struggle, the roadblocks, the searching for food? It was too easy. We even had a nice dinner and breakfast and slept indoors."

"That's the way I roll," laughed Phage. "You like to eke it out, dawdle, and faff about. I'm all about business. Plus, I like riding with Bernard. Usually," she added, pointedly not looking at the big guy. "You always take your bike. It's archaic."

"Hey, I like my bike. And I like the peace." I glared at Bernard. "Plus, you need the cart, so there's enough food for the horn head. And I need time to get into the right mindset. So, what's the plan?"

"The plan is to feed Bernard, you have a smoke, I'll sort out tea, and some food, and then we'll go take a closer look at the castle. What's it called again?"

"Something unpronounceable in Welsh," I mumbled.

"Just feed the unicorn."

"Yes, ma'am." I saluted, then began the arduous job of freeing the aforementioned twatty unicorn. It wasn't the work that was arduous, it was the conversation.

"My hooves are cold."

"Wear socks."

"My nose feels funny."

"It looks it."

"I'm hungry."

"So am I."

"Do you think I'm putting on weight?"

"Yes. You're fat."

"You are so mean."

"I know."

"When can we go home?"

"Never. We're leaving you behind and selling your family to total strangers. For beans. And not even magic ones."

"What's that?"

"Snow."

"Is it night?"

"Yes, but it's light just to confuse you."

"What's digital?"

"Just about everything."

"How long till we get there?"

"You fucking what!?" I blurted, because he was doing my head in.

"Haha, I did a joke." Bernard beamed at me and I couldn't help but laugh.

"You sure did. Damn, how long have you been building up to that?"

"My entire life."

"Haha, wow, two jokes in one day."

"Huh? I only did one."

"Oh, okay. Right, you are free." I sorted out the massive mound of food piled into the cart, laid it out for the old guy to chomp on, then helped Phage sort out our gear. It was minimal, but not as minimal as I liked it. Cold weather was most definitely not a Necro's friend. There were tents, shovels, our packs, blankets, clothes, waterproofs, all manner of crap that was needed. Not good for a fast getaway. But truth be told, if we were alive at the end of this we wouldn't need one. We could take as long as we wanted.

The issue was one of staying hidden until we were ready to act.

I rigged up a tarpaulin a little away from the camp, a brown wall so we were totally hidden and a fire wouldn't be seen. Once that was done, I used the kindling we'd brought with us to light a fire and placed all the brush I'd cleared from our camp next to it to dry off. Then I scoured the area and gathered as much firewood as I could and again set it beside the fire. As the flames took, I fed more on until we had a roaring blaze with little smoke and the air finally began to warm.

Phage made tea on the coals while I moved out of the forest to check we weren't sending smoke signals to whoever we'd come to destroy. There was no sign of us from outside the woods, so that was one thing I didn't have to worry about.

A familiar buzzing came from the west as several drones descended from over the treetops and spied on me. They split up and circled overhead then ventured close and swept the area. Who was watching? Why couldn't they leave us alone? The drones buzzed low and fast, darting to and fro like the annoying bugs they were. Then they shot up and disappeared, leaving me with a dark mood and a cold nose.

I returned to the comfort of the fire and Phage. How I wished she wasn't here. How I was glad she was. It was like sharing a burden, but I feared for her. I feared for myself.

Fiery Friends

"All good," I told Phage as I wandered back into camp.

"We're like ninjas," she laughed.

"I don't like this. It's still too easy to find us."

"Relax. What, do you usually stay totally hidden until you go and you know?"

"Sometimes. Other times I know they're expecting me so I don't even try to hide. It depends."

"On what?" Phage looked genuinely intrigued.

I shrugged. "I just get a feeling. I know if they know, if you know what I mean. Haha, sounds silly. But I get a tingle. I can tell."

"Me too. I have the same thing. And what are your Spidey senses telling you today?"

"That they know we're here. That they don't need to look out of the window. They have other ways of telling. Maybe drones of their own, and the Necrodrones have arrived, by the way. Or maybe they have cameras, or crystal balls. But they're aware."

"That's exactly what I think too. And you said they. That another feeling?"

"Yes, there are a few of them. More than two anyway."

"I get the same sense of it. Soph, this is something different, isn't it? I don't like it."

"No, me neither. This will be unlike anything we've ever done before. And I've done a lot of strange shit. Like, seriously strange."

"Me too. I need to tell you some things. About what I've seen. Odd stuff has happened over the last few years and I don't like it. It's scaring me."

"Hey, it's okay, you can tell me anything. And there's probably more I need to share with you too. To be honest, I'm not even sure what I have told you and what I haven't. All these damn rules about what we're allowed to say messes with my head. Did I tell you about the eyes in the sky? The notes being made and written?"

"You told me. And I've experienced similar. But not just that. Remember when you saw the body at Pam's being taken? You saw the volcano?"

"Yeah. That was a grim night."

"I've caught snippets of similar events over the years. Well, the last four or five years, actually. Glimpses of the Necroverse usually kept hidden. Even from powerful witches like Mother. And some people have given me information I never wanted to hear, too. I can't tell you what, but it's like the world's being slowly unraveled. Or I'm being tested. Like we both are."

"I think that's exactly what's happening. They're showing us what others don't see. Will never see. It's tied up with Jen, I'm sure of it. Because she's special."

"I'm not so sure." Phage bit her lower lip, something Jen had inherited.

"Why? I've been convinced of it, but there's nothing tangible, just what others have said."

"I think it's because of you. Sorry, but it is. You've always been rather self-deprecating when it comes to your abilities, and it's damn annoying at times! You're too cool about what you can do. About how you handle things."

"Me? I'm not cool. I'm a mess."

"No, you aren't. You're tough, you can deal with anything, and your abilities are greater than you ever let on. Your last note, what happened to you in Liverpool with your family, that would have broken any other man."

"Honey, it did break me. I sat there and waited for him to finish me off. I told you that. I was done. Beaten." I moved closer and whispered, "I don't think I should have told you about that. It's against the rules, isn't it?"

Phage whispered back, "I'm not sure anymore. I don't know. You didn't say who he was or what else happened."

We moved apart and continued our conversation.

"Anyway, I was done."

"No, you weren't done. Not at all," said Phage. "And this is exactly what I'm getting at. You say you were beat, that you'd given up, but you hadn't, and you weren't. You called for Bernard, and he saved you, but only because you asked him to. That's not giving in, that's being smart."

"Didn't feel like it at the time. So what are you saying? That you're being shown things because of me? What have you seen?"

"That's the problem. It's nothing, yet I know it means something. It's like I'm being shown individual pieces of a jigsaw puzzle without being given the box and the picture. It's like if I knew what the picture was, the pieces would make sense and I'd know where to put them. But I don't know what I'm supposed to be looking for. I don't know how any of it fits together."

"Damn, you just put into words how I've been feeling for over four years now. That's exactly it. That's precisely how I feel too. So, tell me, what else have you seen or heard?"

"I can't tell you most of it. I know they might be listening. I'm not breaking any rules," Phage said loudly. "But I've seen corpses taken like that Jukel was, although I saw an ocean, not a volcano. I've been confronted with daemons when I've been about to fulfill my note. They were so rude!"

"Yeah, daemons have a habit of being rude." I grinned, but it didn't lighten the mood.

"No, I mean they were *rude* rude. They said the strangest things about me. It was obvious they were trying to put me off. It was a test, I'm sure. Just like you're being tested. That thing in Liverpool, no way that was a coincidence. They could have sent a local. They chose you."

"But why? What's the point?"

"We might never know. Or maybe we will. I just wish it would stop."

"But it won't. It never will."

"I know." Phage's shoulders slumped as though she was about to cry, but she was strong, and had been through this so many times before that she wiped her eyes and they remained dry.

"Come on, let's have that drink."

Phage nodded and made us sweet, steaming tea. We sat by the fire and huddled close for warmth. It was only early afternoon, but it felt as though we'd been here for hours when we hadn't even set up camp properly yet.

We drank in silence as drones buzzed high overhead and our thoughts turned dark, as they so often did when all that confronted you was murder.

Drones scattered as air was forced apart by a powerful creature most humans would have a heart attack if they saw. I smiled.

Tyr alighted in the middle of the fire and folded his large wings. His long neck stretched out and he surveyed the scene with eyes that saw so much more than a human's.

"Tyr is here," he announced, and stared hard at me, like he deserved a round of applause.

"And you're sitting on the kettle," I told him.

Tyr jumped out of the flames and glanced at the offending kettle. I used the glove to retrieve it and he hopped straight back in.

"You shouldn't do that, Tyr," scolded Phage. "We've told you about it."

"Yeah, you could cause a fire. You've been warned lots of times. And look at the size of you now. You're too big to do it. You'll make it go out. Come here. Sit beside us."

"Tyr cold. Not like snow. And drones make head feel strange. More every year. Don't like buzzing. Don't like sneaky spies." He walked lethargically from the fire, so I stoked it then added more wood or we'd have nothing but a smoking mess. It burst into life and Tyr sighed with satisfaction as the temperature rose. He sat with his back to us, staring at the flames, lost in his own world.

Phage and I exchanged a look then I shrugged. Tyr was being odd, even by his standards.

"You took a long time to get here," said Phage. "Was there some kind of a problem?"

Our dragon arched his neck and looked at Phage. "Tyr had to find shelter from storm. Too cold. Brain not work properly. Felt slow and like Tyr would fall. Tyrant of the Sky needs heat to work properly. Had to feed lots, but animals hide when cold."

"Well, we're glad you made it." I turned to Phage and repeated what Tyr had said.

"We are," she agreed. "Is your head feeling better now?"

He nodded, then returned to gazing into the flames. Guess he was trying to activate his brain cells, as unlike Bernard, he genuinely did slow down if he got too cold. We sat and waited while Tyr gradually came back to life.

He began to twitch, his color returned after being a drab brown, and even his ridges slowly seemed to become more erect. His scales rippled as the incredible temperature soaked into his thick hide and I wondered if this was how he would be in a few years. Would he lose his fun side? Be dark, brooding, and mysterious? Communicate less and less as he moved to adulthood? I knew enough about dragons to understand they were very different to us, but so far Tyr had been on a par with Jen. Their formative years were comparable in many ways.

But he was changing rapidly now he was approaching what I had imagined to be his teenage years. I had got it wrong. His progression was no longer like Jen's. After feeding for the second time, something had switched inside his head. He was more grown up than her. Tyr was becoming an adult.

There was plenty of growing left, but he was maturing rapidly and I had to adjust how I treated him or there would be trouble.

"How are you feeling now, Tyr?" I asked.

"Tyr can think. Warmer. You kill today?"

I told Phage what he asked and we exchanged another look. Damn, he was serious today.

"Not today. At least that isn't the plan. But we'll see. Why?"

"Tyr must feed soon. Needs blood. Necro blood."

"We've discussed this. Hang on, let me tell Phage. He wants to feed on a Necro. Says he needs it."

"No, you aren't allowed. You know what you read in the book. You must wait longer. You have fed twice. Once on a Necro, once on a regular human. That's enough for now. It is, isn't it, Soph?"

"Yes. You don't need more yet. Tyr, look at us." He shifted his body and faced us. Those eyes of his were intense. I saw the craving, the addiction. He really wanted this. "It's too soon. You fed just months ago. The book said wait. We must wait."

"Tyr not like other dragons. Tyr is special. Different."

"That's news to me. How are you different? And what other dragons have you met? As far as I know there aren't any in this country."

For the longest time, Tyr simply stared at me, unblinking, then he turned his attention to Phage and repeated the stare.

"Tyr knows because he has powers that the book says are for older dragons. Tyr reads you. Knows you. I know the truth when you speak. I know lies. I know doubt and I know your fear."

"That's supposed to happen much later. But nothing is set in stone. You all grow differently." Again, I repeated what he'd said for Phage.

"Do you mean like a Constable?" she asked. "You can read our faces, how we move, see what they see? Like a sorcerer maybe?"

"Tyr sees things when he looks at hands, or eyes, or mouth. Tyr knows Phage's thoughts, Soph's too. Sees everything. Tyr must feed." He turned away from us again and watched the flickering flames.

"We're going to take a little walk. Tyr, you guard the camp. We won't be long."

"Tyr knows you go to talk about him."

I nodded to Phage and we left camp.

"Blimey, that was weird and unsettling. He's changed a lot."

"Jen said the same thing," agreed Phage. "She said when she visits him he knows what she's been doing and what she has planned. Like he can see the future."

"It's not actually seeing it like a seer, is it? It's, um, what's the word? Ah, extrapolating. Kind of what sorcerers do, what Constables do. It's freaky though. Haha, we better watch what we say around him now."

"Is it magic, or is it like a Constable? Although, I guess there's magic in that too."

"Yeah, but they go through years of training. They have a gift for it, sure, but it's the training."

"That's the same as sorcerers. They train too. What's the difference between the two?"

"Sorcerers call on magic, on the Necroverse to help them. They sink into it, see futures that way. It's not reading body language, it's getting visions of the future from what someone does in the present then kind of following it through the Necroverse. Um, I think. Hey, you should know more about it than me. You know this isn't my thing."

"I know witches. I know how they do things. The old ones, the visionaries, they are like sorcerers, but I think Tyr might be more like a mix of everything."

"I think you're right. He's special, even by dragon standards. Did you see the way he looked at us? He's got smart too. Real smart."

"Dragons are more intelligent than humans. A lot more. We've got to keep him close, and we need to get him a new house. Soph, that should be a priority when we get home."

"I'll sort it. Promise. A massive steel barn so he can come and go as he pleases."

Phage nodded. "I think we should go and take a look at the castle. See what we're up against."

"Tyr can come?"

We jumped at his voice. Neither of us had heard him approach. And as we turned, then stood mute with shock, it was obvious why.

"Bloody hell, Tyr, you're a man. That man."

"How did you do that? Look at you. I didn't think you could hold the form."

"Tyr has been locked up for long time. Practiced skills. Tyr can be man, two men, can be dog. Tyr is best friends with Jen. Jen has powers. Tyr wants powers too. Lots of adventures. And Tyr can be man for Jen. We can be married like Soph and Phage."

"We'll talk about that when you are much older. And I mean a lot older. Jen is a child and so are you. Yes, I know you've grown up quite a bit, but you are still young. And Tyr?"

"Yes?"

"You are a dragon. You cannot remain a person. You cannot be with a human. You cannot be with Jen in that way."

"Tyr will practice being a man. Jen will need a husband."

"What's he saying? What's that about Jen?" Phage was full of concern, and as freaked out as I was.

"He wants to marry her. To look after her. Damn, this is getting complicated all of a sudden."

Phage moved closer to Tyr and looked him up and down, his naked body pale, almost blue with the cold. "You cannot marry her, Tyr. I know you love her, and she loves you too. But dragons and people cannot be together in that way. Do you understand?"

"Tyr understand." He nodded so Phage would see. "But Tyr will practice. Look, I can move like man." He walked back and forth, coordination perfect. How did he do that? How did he know how to use a human body so well? Guess he really had been practicing.

"Well done, but I think it's best you return to your normal body now," I told him. "You're freezing and you will be burning a lot of energy. Save the morph for when it's necessary, okay?"

"Tyr is cold," he agreed. With a nod, he turned and began walking away, then dropped to all fours partway, and shifted back into dragon form with ease. It was impressive, and beyond worrying.

"That's all we need. It hadn't even crossed my mind he'd get an idea like that into his head."

"He can't be with Jen in that way," whispered Phage. "He's a dragon. They can't, can they?"

"No, absolutely not. Gotta hand it to the guy though, he's determined."

"And that's a worry. Jen's young and impressionable. If Tyr convinces her to..."

"No, not on my watch. That is not going to happen. You ever hear of anything like this? I sure haven't."

"Soph, you are centuries older than me but sometimes I swear you don't know a thing about the Necroverse."

"I know more than I want to. Well?"

"Yes, I've heard of it. Not for a long time, as we aren't exactly overrun with dragons. But it has happened."

"And what was the outcome?"

"What do you think?"

"They lived happily ever after?"

"No. They didn't."

"Didn't think so. Right, let's go take a look at the big, looming castle on the hill, shall we? This is crazy. Wonder what the deal is?"

Phage took my hand. "Let's go find out, shall we?" I was about to move when she said, "Wait."

"What is it?"

"Um, I know I laughed, but do you think maybe we should take some of the power pellets? Just a bit?"

"Power pellets? Oh, you mean Tyr's poo?"

"I prefer power pellets. It sounds less..."

"Disgusting? Gross? A foul thing to do?" I winked at my reddening wife.

"Yes. That. It's so annoying not being able to understand the animals, and it might help with that and who knows what else. Just a boost. What harm can it do?"

"I have absolutely no idea. But it didn't hurt Jen, and Woofer can't get enough of the stuff. Okay, let's do it." I removed my pack and broke off two large pieces, then crushed it between our knives until it was a very rough powder. We both stuffed it into our mouths then took in turns swigging the stuff down with several gulps of water.

"What are you feeling?" asked Phage.

"Nothing but unclean."

"It doesn't taste of much."

"Guess that's because it's dried. Okay, you ready?"

"No, but there's no choice."

We headed towards the castle, geared up, ready for anything. But in our world, anything really could mean anything, and who can be prepared for all our world can throw at them?

Unknown Enemies

We skirted the castle at a distance, but if we wished to remain hidden we weren't going to see much of anything. There was no sign of life, but it was hardly surprising. After all, it was a bloody big castle with thick walls, turrets, towers, and damn high.

It sat proudly atop a hill so steep that it had never been breached, had remained mostly intact all these centuries. It wasn't the largest of its kind, but it was still huge, and easily defended from any angle.

The only good thing about its position from our perspective was that over time the forests around its base had spread, providing cover. Off to the north, pasture still remained, now home to herds of deer that roamed freely, which was apparent from the damage we could already see. It looked like they would decimate the new growth trying to fight its way through the competition, and soon, if the caretakers of our historic buildings and lands weren't careful, there'd be nothing left of the gardens, and ancient woodlands would slowly decline, then die.

The trees provided good cover as we investigated the perimeter, searching for the best access, with several overgrown paths to choose from. Continuing around, we finally made it to the once-formal gardens at the very base of the castle and hid behind scruffy yew no longer clipped into neat whimsical shapes.

From here, the view to the castle was unrestricted, so we settled down for a while to simply watch. Patience was needed here, and yet I was itching to move, to get this done. No lights, no movement, no nothing. It could be unoccupied; it could be full of people.

Once we felt the time was right, we moved through trees and wild rhododendrons, the castle hidden from view by a series of steep terraces that once would dazzle thousands of daily visitors with their botanical displays. Now the going was treacherous as the paths and countless steps were hidden under the deep snow.

We climbed several tiers until we could see the entrance. The twisting road came up from an old car park for the visitors that used to arrive daily in droves. Cars, coaches full of sight-seers, walkers, it would have thronged with happy people out for a day trip not so long ago. Now it was crumbling away, just like everything else.

The road turned to a path, then stopped at the large portico. The heavy wooden doors were open. Two narrow towers loomed either side, perfect for an ambush. Through the gap we spied a small lawned courtyard. Cobbled paths writhed around and across the grass, leading to numerous small entrances to various parts of the castle. In direct line with the portico, a series of grand, wide steps led to an impressive double entrance with two more towers where guards would have once been stationed, ready to shoot an arrow in your eye or drop a rock on your head if you were naughty.

A statue in the middle of the courtyard pointed to the sky, but I couldn't make out the figure very well, or recall who it was meant to be, just that it was a woman on horseback, maybe holding a lance or a flag. Possibly a sword. I had visited here several times over the years, in different guises, walked around the gardens and the lavish interiors. It wasn't the largest castle by any means, but the paintings were impressive, the towers a delight, and the ice cream served from a small kiosk on the bottom terrace had been memorable on a warm summer's day.

The entire estate had thronged with families out for adventure. There was picnicking, kids running, playing tag, everyone smiling, admiring the plants, commenting on the sheer scale of the undertaking to build atop such a steep hill. The views were incredible, a panoramic three-sixty that made the location perfect for marveling at the beauty of the Welsh countryside. Or lording it over the peasants if you'd lived here when it was first built.

Now it was just us.

A peacock called from the courtyard. They'd been here back then too, and had obviously managed to hang on even without the care of the volunteers. Maybe the people here now looked after them. Somehow, I didn't think so.

I raised my eyebrows at Phage.

She nodded.

It was game on.

I have often wondered over the years if I have a death wish. I usually do little in the way of planning, as I need to know what I'm facing and the element of surprise is hardly ever on my side. So I front it out, knock on doors, ring bells, shout a hearty hello, then stab them in the face. Was it just me?

As Phage stood from her crouched position and marched towards the open portico, I finally understood I was not alone in my bravado, or stupidity. She strode confidently forward and I ran quickly to join her. Here we were, two Necros about to meet unknown forces, walking straight into who knew what?

Either they knew we were coming or they didn't, so we were either already tracked and they were waiting, or they didn't suspect a thing.

At the huge studded wooden door, easily fifteen feet tall, we leaned back either side of the entrance and took in the courtyard. It was empty save for the peacock pecking around in slushy snow. Several paths had been cleared leading from one door to the other and the main entrance was clear. Mounds of dirty snow were banked up either side, and numerous footsteps criss-crossed grass blackened by the harsh weather.

How many people were here? How many were our enemies?

With a nod, we both took a side and skirted around the edge of the courtyard. The peacock wasn't even remotely interested in us. We made it to the steps and took them slowly, careful not to slip on ice, ever vigilant. Inside the open doors, a large foyer with a thick grill in the floor announced the wealth of the old occupants. I peered down into the void but saw nothing but darkness. What was this for? A drain? Why was I bothering with it now? I snapped out of it and turned to peer into the stately rooms off to the right. Ahead, three tiers of steps led down into an enclosed rear courtyard, if I remembered rightly. I pointed to the right and we stepped inside.

A body lay crumpled next to the empty fireplace on the left. Dried blood clung to the mantelpiece, a stain on its history. A woman with dark hair, smashed glasses, and a terrible gouge out of her forehead stared at us accusingly. Her face, particularly around her cheeks and mouth, was blackened by severe burns. She was dead. She still clutched a file in her right hand. It was scorched too. My guess was she'd been a volunteer looking after the place. There was no trace of anyone else, no sound, and the kill was relatively fresh, so whoever had done this hadn't been here for more than a few days. Unless it was another volunteer who'd killed her, which didn't seem very likely.

We followed the path along rugs larger than a conventional house, keeping to the route the rope rails directed. The rooms were still in prime condition, nothing smashed, nothing taken, no paintings torn from walls. No looters, in other words. That meant the security teams were still active here, as the ransacking of such treasure troves had been rife when our world first changed. These places were easy pickings. It soon stopped when private security firms were employed and the government gave them the right to use firearms and protect the properties. Still, it should have been locked up at the moment, so something wasn't quite right here.

We found the security in the next room. Three men with their hands and feet bound and their heads basically chewed off.

"What the fuck?" I mouthed to Phage. She shook her head. She had no idea. Something very large had gnawed on the faces of these unfortunates, and I wouldn't have been surprised to discover they were alive while it happened.

"Oh my god, oh my god," screamed a woman as she ran towards us in a panic, arms flapping, a file in one hand. Her glasses slid down her nose and she pushed them back up then brushed a curly lock from her eyes.

I morphed without hesitation and came up right behind her even as she continued running. As the pain hit, I eased the knife into her kidney, twisted it sharply to the right, then yanked it hard left as I turned my body around her to increase the force. I felt the edge hit bone and I thrust deeper again then clamped my arm over her mouth before her scream even began. She slumped forward, her momentum almost gone, and the blade slid free easily as her spinal column was severed. Once she was prone, I flipped her over instantly then slid the knife between her ribcage and punctured her heart. Blood pumped through her thick cardigan and soaked my leather glove as I pulled the knife out with a rasp against her bones. I wiped the long blade on her legs, and as I grunted and stood she soiled herself.

The entire incident took two seconds max.

"I know an evil bitch when I see one," I told Phage. And then what I'd done in front of my wife hit me like a punch to the guts. A wave of shame washed over me. Would she still love me? Could I ever look her in the eyes again? I hung my head. This was the first woman I had ever killed. Yet I had acted immediately. Why? Because my wife's safety was paramount. I absolutely wouldn't let her be harmed. If that meant losing what few morals remained, then so be it. When Pam was attacked, I'd hesitated to kill her enemy. I would not make the same mistake twice. Yet I felt dirty, wrong. Men shouldn't kill women; it wasn't right. I couldn't help how I felt. It just wasn't right.

Phage took my bloodied hands and, reluctantly, I lifted my head and met her kind, loving eyes.

"You were wonderful," she whispered. "You did the right thing. You didn't even pause. That was impressive." She kissed me. "How did you know?" she asked, quickly glancing up and down the room to ensure nobody else was coming.

"She wasn't out of breath, or sweating. It was too convenient. And her clipboard was empty. Just a prop. But it was the glasses that gave her away. They didn't fit her head. She took them from someone else. Which means there are more dead innocents here somewhere. What's with these guys with their faces chewed off? What did that?"

We both turned from each other and stared at the poor men. They would be unrecognizable, even to their families.

"It wasn't Tyr, but it was something bloody big. Guess we'll find out. Soph, that was amazing. Truly. I don't mean it wasn't horrible," she added hurriedly, "but I didn't know you were a detective as well as my hero." She pecked me on the cheek again before we moved on to the next room.

Should I feel bad, or should I feel glad my wife was okay with what I'd done? Being impressed by someone's murder technique is not something you expect to feel about a partner for life. At least, not normal people. But we were Necro, and I guess that's exactly the kind of person you do want by your side.

I called out to Tyr and Bernard as we walked. I told Bernard to hang tight, and stay hidden, and asked Tyr to circle the castle and see what he could discover. Both were grumpy, monosyllabic, but it was tough shit. They could bloody well earn their keep.

"What do you think this is?" I asked Phage.

"No idea. But she wasn't exactly hard to kill, no offense, so my guess is she was a sacrificial lamb. A servant maybe."

"A servant?"

"You know, a trainee. The dogsbody. An acolyte sent to test the waters. Earn her stripes."

"She was in her forties."

"Where have you been all this time? In our world, the world of witches, you can be treated like crap for a long, long time. Until you can prove yourself. But I might be wrong. It could be you just got the better of her before she could do anything."

"Yeah, maybe. But I think you're right. Come on, let's finish this. Whatever this is."

The dust of centuries tickled my nostrils as we scouted several more rooms, found another two dead bodies, one male, one female, but thankfully this time they'd been dispatched rapidly. A quick slit of the throat. Deep and deadly. Finally we made it to the main stairway after we'd circled back around the building in a rather convoluted way. A red carpet led the way up. It was wet with numerous footmarks, so others were definitely here and had been active for some time. Down was just as wet and muddy, but there was no carpet. We headed that way first.

The servants' quarters were vastly different to the extravagance of above. Bare walls, no carpets or rugs, next to no decoration, and purely functional. We found a series of bedrooms, the huge kitchen, and plenty of storage areas. All of it was how it would have been when the place was a tourist attraction, the rooms laid out to show how life was lived here in the past. Nothing was used or had been disturbed recently. It was a museum, nothing more.

We continued cautiously along the curved corridor, then Phage suddenly stopped and put a finger to her lips. She pressed her ear against the lime-washed wall then stepped back and gently rested her palms on the freezing stone.

"There's a room the other side. This isn't a real wall."

"Looks real enough to me." I rapped on it with my knuckles. "Feels real too."

Phage shook her head then placed her palms back onto the wall. She closed her eyes and began to whisper. I quickly placed my hands over my ears to allow her to keep her secrets, to keep private words she'd spent so many years mastering. The energy levels in the corridor rocketed instantly. I felt the strength of her magic, the hardly tamed wildness, the focus and the intent.

Her whispers intensified. Dark wisps of matter twisted and slithered from her mouth as she spoke words I could not hear and would not understand anyway. The silent tendrils caressed the wall, searching for a way in, and then they were sucked through tiny air pockets between the stonework. Suddenly, the wall was no longer a wall, but a door. On a simple brass hook beside it hung a large, old-fashioned key like a jailer would use. This wasn't a room, it was a cell.

Phage peered through the narrow slit in the ancient, studded door then stepped back and motioned for me to take a look.

"A tiger? What is going on in this place?"

"No idea. We need to speak to him." I took the key and unlocked the door. It creaked as I opened it. I winced, wondering if the sound would reach the ears of those we'd been tasked with murdering. Did it matter?

The room stank. The tiger cowered away into the corner, head low. I remained where I was while I took in the layout of the room. There wasn't much to see. It was damp, it was covered in urine and shit that had clearly been building for months, and all the poor creature had by way of comfort was a small pile of rancid straw in a corner. A large, barred window ventilated the room somewhat, but it also made it absolutely freezing as this was the north side.

"Hey, it's okay. Don't be scared." I glanced back at Phage who remained in the doorway, not wanting to spook the animal.

"Don't hurt me." The large beast backed further into the corner until it's rear was pressed against the sopping wall, and tried to make himself as small as possible. Poor thing was petrified.

"I won't hurt you. I would never do that. If you look at me, you will see that I am not your enemy. I'm your friend. We're both your friends. Do you want me to take that off your neck?" A large, thick leather collar with a D-ring connected to a heavy chain bolted to the flagstone floor was tight around its furry neck, but it had rubbed the matted fur away and dug into the skin, creating a ring of raw, infected flesh. A ring of shame. Shame on those who would mistreat such a regal, beautiful, innocent creature in this manner.

"It hurts, but I am used to it now. Been so long. So many years. You will free me? Why?" he asked suspiciously. The heavy chain rattled as he slid guardedly along the wall. It dragged on the floor, more like a chain used on an anchor than to restrain a tiger. Oversized purely to inflict misery and keep the creature's head cowed before a cruel, malicious master.

I wanted to scream. To tear the cell apart with my bare hands. To pound to mush the head of the bastard who thought this was acceptable.

"Why? Because you don't want to be chained up. Because it's cruel and a terrible thing to do. Do you want your freedom? I will give it to you."

"Freedom? What is freedom? Do not know the word."

"It's being able to do what you want. To not be locked up, or treated badly. To be fed regularly, be clean, see the outside world."

"The world out there, through the window?" He looked at the white world beyond the castle walls.

"Yes. Mind you, we don't have tigers roaming loose in the country. You'll have to come home with us, live with the other animals. But you won't be harmed. You will be protected and safe. So, it's freedom, but you still need to hide from other humans to keep yourself protected."

"Not free then. Just another prison. Please don't beat me."

He whined and hung his head so low I wanted to rush to him and rip off the collar. But I had to take this slow, and not spook him. He may have been cowed and timid, but a wild, cornered animal is always dangerous.

"We won't hurt you," soothed Phage as she moved cautiously across the room. "I can hear him," she told me, smiling a little. "It's so strange. Is he actually talking out loud?"

"Kind of. Lots of it is mental, but if you couldn't understand it would be like always. You'd hear some tiger growls and that's about it. You okay with this?"

"It's weird, but yes, I like it." Phage turned back to the tiger and told him again, "We will never hurt you."

"I'm always being abused. Kicked and beaten and scolded. Told I am bad. Always."

"That's over now. We will give you a home. Do you know what that means?" she asked.

"Yes. Home is where you live. Live here. This is home."

"No, this isn't home. This is a prison. There is a big difference. We will care for you, and nobody will ever hurt you again. We won't hurt you. We are your friends."

"That's right. We're your friends," I agreed. "We will feed you, ensure you're comfortable, and never hurt you. My daughter would love to brush your fur. She'll tell you stories and get out all the matts until you shine as bright as the sun."

"Do you want that?"

"Yes."

"Okay, then let's get you out of here and then we can all leave."

"My masters won't allow it."

"Then we'll have to kill them, won't we?" I told him. I held his gaze as his head lifted at the words.

"No, mustn't kill them. Not allowed. Is bad."

"So is what they're doing to you. We have to kill them and we have to get you away. Do you understand that?"

"Yes."

"If you don't want to hurt anyone, that's fine. We will do what's to be done and then we will all leave. Together. Okay?"

He nodded his head. I moved closer to him very slowly, no sudden movements, aware how jittery he was. He was beginning to trust us. I just had to play it cool and not startle him.

"Now, I'm just going to release this clasp and then the collar will come free. It will be loud, and it might make you jump, but it's nothing to worry about. When was the last time it came off?"

He stared at me, confused. "Never comes off. Maybe when I was young it was changed when I grew, but always have the collar on."

"Okay, I understand. It will feel strange at first then, but you are going to love it. You can move freely. Why are you here?"

"Pet. I was told I was a pet. But it isn't true. They used me."

"What did they use you for?"

"Bad things." His head hung low but I reached out slowly and put my hand under his chin and lifted up so he was looking at me.

"That's all over with now. You can tell us when you're ready. Right, here we go." I fumbled with the chain attached by a thick pin, and once it was free I laid it as carefully as I could onto the floor. It was so heavy I was amazed he'd been able to keep his head up at all. I couldn't even imagine the strain on his neck. I released a catch and then the collar was off. His neck was in a terrible state. It must have hurt so badly. Had he ever known a day without suffering? I lowered the collar to the dirty ground and then stepped back to stand beside Phage.

"How does that feel?" she asked, smiling sweetly at our new friend.

He shook out his entire body from tip to tail and then twisted his head from side to side. He kept his eyes on us at all times, wary, but not as cowed as he'd been. Then he stretched his neck up high and sighed.

"It feels light! My head is weightless. I can move. I can move!" With that, he bounded up then landed in a crouch and hissed. "They must pay for what they have done, but I am afraid. They hurt me so much for so long. I cannot kill. I must never kill. They made me. I had to kill those men. I ate their faces. My masters beat me until I did what they wanted. I didn't want to. He made me. He has power. He twisted into my head and forced me."

"That's good you don't want to hurt anyone," I told him. "But we have to do some bad things to escape, but they are not your friends. They are not good people. We will help you but you must warn us if anyone comes. Help us so we can help you."

"I will."

"What's your name?" asked Phage.

"Rocky."

"Pleased to meet you, Rocky. I'm Phage. This is Soph."

"Hello Phage. Hello Soph. Thank you."

"Great to meet you too, Rocky. You good to go?"

"I am ready. Scared, but ready."

With a nod to Phage, we exited the cell and continued to search the castle. This could take forever. Then I realized something, and stopped in the freezing corridor.

"Check the Necroapp. It will have them marked, I bet. It gives precise locations. Maybe it will show us where they all are."

Phage nodded, then messed with her phone for a few seconds until the app was up and running. How come hers always worked first time and mine was so stubborn? Maybe I didn't press the screen the right way? We were in a bloody castle and she still got a connection. It just wasn't fair.

"Nothing. Just the castle in general. It should show us, but it doesn't."

"Then we split up, do a search."

"Soph, I think we should stick together. I think we need to."

"No problem. Come on, let's go and finish this."

"I can help. What do you need to know?" asked Rocky.

"Who is here? How long have they been here? Who are they? Where were they before this?"

"So many questions," Rocky whined, clearly uncomfortable and not quite with it after his ordeal.

"Just do your best," Phage told him.

"There is only one man. My master. I have been with him many years. I don't know how many. Since a cub. He took me from another. A kind woman. He killed her."

"So he's alone?"

"No. He has others who do his bidding. Women who would follow him. Some he has killed, others still do as he wishes. We came here months ago. He hid me away. Others came. Guards. People who cleaned and repaired. He hid too while they were here, but at night he would emerge and taunt me. Prowl the castle, do his terrible things."

"What things?"

"His work. His terrible, cruel work."

"Can you tell us?" asked Phage kindly. "Please be quick. He might be coming."

"He breaks things, places, goes through the cracks. I don't understand it. It is magic. Master slips away into other places and he says he is close, can almost get to the source."

"The source of what?"

"The notes."

Phage and I exchanged a look. It was bloody obvious why we were here then.

"That's great, Rocky. You've been a real help. I promise we will talk a lot more once this is over. But rest assured, you are free. Nobody will ever put a collar and chain on you again, my friend."

"You really have been a great help," agreed Phage. "Do you know where he is? Where the others are? How many?"

"He has three women with him. They adore him, do whatever he says. I think he controls their minds somehow." He sniffed and then said, "One is dead. Two more are upstairs. I do not know where master is."

"That's awesome. Thank you, Rocky. Hey, don't suppose you gave yourself that name, did you?"

Rocky grinned. His teeth were yellow; his breath was terrible. "I saw the movie as a cub. I wanted to be just like him."

"Sweet."

"What movie?" asked Phage.

"I forget how young you are sometimes. When we get home, you're in for a treat," I told her. "Right, come on, let's go hunting."

Harsh Truths

Rocky was cautious, timid, afraid, and bloody massive. Even with his cowed body language, his terrible wound, and his crusty, greasy, lank fur, he was a sight that would impress. He was large even by tiger standards. I could only imagine how he'd look when he was fed properly. Currently, he was all skin and bone, with little in the way of true muscle. We'd soon put that right.

We moved up the stairs in a line, him slightly behind in the middle, Phage and I ready for whatever. I held my knife at my side, the ebony handle a comfort. Phage favored a much shorter weapon than mine, but I knew she could handle it like a pro.

Tyr checked in and reported no signs of movement, but that he got a sense of several people in the east tower. I thanked him and he said he would return to the fire.

We continued our climb, increasingly cautious the higher we went. Rocky followed the scent, then directed us around the landing towards the tower Tyr had told me about.

I stopped and asked Rocky, "Why did you all come here? Where were you before that? Why this place?"

"Master needed the height. He said it helped with his work. To channel his power, enter the places no one should enter. I don't understand how, but he said it was necessary. We hid until nightfall yesterday, then he killed the others and became so nasty and cruel. More than ever. He beat me so bad. Will you kill him?"

"Yes, we will."

"Good."

We eased along a large hallway-cum-room lined with paintings. The floor shone as the light reflected through numerous windows. It smelled musty and of the past. Another time, another world. Once, it would have been full of people running the castle. Always busy, always things to do. Now there was just us and the corpses.

I stopped dead in my tracks the moment Phage and Rocky did. We spread out in the expansive room, easily twenty feet wide and a hundred long, and watched the two women as they walked brazenly towards us. Both wore cheap, functional brown work clothes, but it belied their powers. I could practically taste the magic oozing out of them, same as the woman I'd just killed. A bitter tang on my tongue. Corrupt and cruel.

"Rocky, you can leave now. We can handle this. Go and wait somewhere safe. We'll catch you up later," I told him.

"I will stay. I will do what I can. So much killing, so much death, but they deserve a terrible end."

"We hear you, pathetic cat!" spat the woman opposite me. Both had long dark hair, probably early forties, were thin and jittery like addicts, but they had power and not of the nice kind.

"You beat me! You kicked me! You made me do those terrible things to so many people. You entered my head and forced me. It hurt so bad but you didn't care."

"Why should we?" laughed the other, her eyes dancing with mirth. "You're pathetic. So weak."

"Wow, you two are just lovely, aren't you?" I said, checking to see if Phage was ready.

She nodded.

As the women opened their mouths to reply, we both morphed and came up behind our counterpart. My knife was already moving, but as the pain took hold of me and I forced myself to focus, she'd vanished. Both women appeared ten feet in front of us, hands rising as their whispers filled the air.

"No fucking chance," I shouted, and morphed again. I materialized above my mark, my knife clutched tight as I fell like a grumpy stone. She looked up in shock as I slammed into her and stabbed into her left shoulder. She hissed and was gone, but I'd got a hit in.

Ding, ding. Round two.

I spun, ready for her to attack from behind, but she was back down the room, close to the other woman.

Phage screamed as her shifting ability took her over and she became something truly not of this world.

Her bones cracked. Limbs fattened and stretched. My adorable wife's head expanded, the skull thickened, dainty, perfect ears became two large lumps of misshapen clay, but her nose almost vanished and her eyes sank deep beneath thick brows. Phage's entire body turned a deep brown while her muscles ballooned in impossible ways, becoming larger than even the modern Mr. Olympias—where drug use had become so extreme they no longer even resembled human beings. Neither did Phage.

Phage had been scared to show me for a very long time, worrying I would think less of her, fearing I'd be disgusted. I saved my disgust for the deeds I'd committed, the man I'd become, not someones else's appearance. Especially not the woman I loved. She'd cried with relief when I told her as much, saying it was the first time in her life she'd felt accepted for who she truly was. Then she'd demonstrated what else she could do, and that was probably even scarier. A lot more fun though.

I darted back and forth between the two women as Phage changed, taunting them but unable to do more than cut them a little. They were fast, but I kept them away from Phage for the few seconds it took her shift to complete.

And then the monster roared. Her cry bounced off the dark paneled walls and into the hearts and minds of our enemies. Phage thundered down the hall, whispering her words as misshapen feet pounded the floor, stopping the two women from morphing for valuable seconds.

I charged the one in front of me as Phage singled out the other.

Deep into it now, I focused on what I had to do, not Phage's actions or the danger she faced. Zero distraction. With the witch's whispers little but weak, pitiful nagging at my mind, I ran at her, ready to finish this and get to the main course. I reached out and hooked her around the neck with my left hand while swinging her, hoping to bring my knife in and finish this fast. She backhanded me and turned away sharply, forcing me to change tactic and kick her legs out instead. With my grip holding, we dropped as one.

A dirty fighter is a winning fighter, and those who believe in, and abide by, rules of combat die young, so I tore her ear off with my teeth as I stabbed like I was digging the dirt. Over and over, wild and frenzied, a berserker fool without a mind, just intent on death. I felt her whispers, felt her tense and knew she would morph, so I rolled aside as she appeared not two feet away on what would have been my left, her knife already moving to finish me.

My leg kicked out and I got a good boot into her knee but there was no satisfying crack as I'd expected. My aim off just enough. She sneered, spiteful and full of contempt, then spread her arms as her whispers deepened because Phage had clearly lost her hold over both women. But I still paid Phage no heed. I had my own battle to fight and remained focused.

I called to the inhabitants of this castle. The mice and the rats, the spiders and the bugs, the flies and the insects all around. However, winter is no time for spiders to acknowledge the call of a zoolinguist—most were dead or hiding away, barely alive. But the mice and rats came at my behest, scampered from their winter retreats and scurried along corridors, emerged from cracks in walls, ascended from the basement and tapped along the floorboards like a hundred horses racing towards us. In moments, a tidal wave of tiny furry creatures heeded my request and engulfed both women.

They screamed and they hollered as countless tiny teeth took minuscule lumps of flesh as their prize. Death by a thousand bites was my expectation. But it was never that easy.

The rats chewed, clinging to the bodies of both women, scrabbling at the door they protected. My insistent urging sent them into a frenzy as they gnawed and scratched at the women and the ancient oak as hard as iron. They clambered over each other to build tiny ladders of writhing mayhem, searching for a way into the room beyond, as all the while more and more emerged from their slumber and joined the witch party.

My mark batted at the creatures, muffled screams and wild eyes giving me a moment to compose myself and check on Phage. She was going apeshit on her opponent, the mice and rats keeping low, attacking her legs while Phage swung weighted punch after weighted punch at the woman who cackled and ducked the swings that would destroy her with a single blow if one connected.

The acolyte was anticipating the moves, could read them, so Phage changed tack. She simply lunged for the woman, then turned with a sleight, slid into her legs, and toppled the crone. The rodents bristled and became utterly manic. They tore and ripped at clothes and flesh. They bit and gnawed, chewed and defecated on Phage's mark as she scrambled about on the floor, the sheer volume of creatures upon her clearly making her seer abilities impossible to control.

All this was taken in with a glance and then I focused on my own opponent who was strangely still, yet covered in the creatures. Her whispers strengthened, insinuating themselves into my mind, reaching out, trying to break my control over my helpful little friends. I held fast, pushed with all my mental ability, and held on to my link with a thousand furry saviors.

Her magic was weak, I could fight it, but first the mice, then the rats slowed their attack as the ferocity of the whispers increased. They fought back, nibbling and scratching, but I couldn't keep up the required intensity to get them to destroy the damn women.

Then for a moment, their power waned, their whispers slid on by, and those under my command let loose in a flurry of manic raking of flesh and tearing with teeth and I was buoyed by their newfound strength. I redoubled my efforts, but something told me to stop, to change direction and put my mental focus on another issue. A bloody big and scary one.

I felt the whispers tear at the poor, beaten creature behind us, cowering in a corner, afraid of the wildness that raged. I spoke to him, told him to remain calm and all was well even though I knew it was anything but. As I tried to impress upon him the need to remain focused, the whispers of both witches combined into one mighty command of intent and Rocky was unable to resist.

I turned and saw him rise from his bowed position to stand tall and proud. His eyes stuttered madly, all awareness gone from those soft, caring orbs. Replaced with a madness. A bloodlust. A desire, no, a need, to kill.

"Fight it! Fight it as hard as you can, my friend. We are here for you, but you must stay in control."

"I am... It is... Will you love me?"

"I will. We will. You will have many new friends. I promise you." I wept for Rocky as I knew he was lost. He didn't hear my promise. He was gone and the witches had taken over.

I checked on Phage. She was back in her own body. Naked, bruised, fighting with every ounce of her being to stop the whispers of her foe. But Phage's own whispers were strong and overpowering, and her opponent faltered. Encouraged, Phage stabbed out with her knife and caught the woman in the shoulder. As the witch hissed and clapped, sending a shockwave through Phage that almost toppled her, I knew we had to do something or we would be devoured.

"Phage, multiply," I shouted.

She nodded, and then there were two Phages. She split again. Now there were four. Then again. Eight.

The witches were confused. I took advantage and reaffirmed my desire for the faltering rodents to destroy these women. They redoubled their efforts and swarmed over the faces of the women as Phage spread out, four of her in front of one four behind the other.

Her body was solid, nothing else was. Weapons were an illusion, but what did that matter when eight of her clawed, punched, kicked, smashed, and gouged while the true Phage stabbed at the witch with a head covered in rats and mice as they gnawed her eyeballs and slid into her gaping maw?

The woman dropped. Phage, naked and utterly glorious in her madness, lost to the bloodlust, stabbed into the heart of the woman and she stilled.

Sixteen murderous eyes turned to the other witch, and as the woman wailed, lamenting the loss of her sister in cruelty, I ordered the smaller mice to slip into her mouth.

Rocky roared in anguish as he pelted towards us, and I turned in time to see him launch at me. I ducked, and he sailed overhead. Claws raked my shoulder and scalp, but I felt nothing. I was too consumed with bloodlust for that. The tiger smashed into the witch just as her whispers were cut off by the scurrying mice, and as he tumbled away I sprang forward. With my knife gripped tightly in both hands, I thrust the blade into the woman's neck so hard it went clean through her windpipe, then her spinal column, and stuck fast into the floor beneath.

I yanked hard, my energy waning, and pulled the blade free. Blood spurted for a moment, soaking my face and head, and then I dropped back onto my ass and sat there, panting. I rubbed the blood from my eyes with my free hand, aware I would look utterly deranged. I felt filthy to my core.

The rodents stopped their insanity and I thanked them silently then released them and apologized for my intrusion.

A carpet of brown and silver rolled away in ripples down the hall; silence fell like night in a desert. Fast, cold, and complete.

I turned my aching, bruised head to watch the multiples of Phage vanish, leaving my wife straddling the witch. The knife still clutched tight, her knuckles white. She stared at the blade numbly, as though she had just awoken from a terrible dream. I knew the feeling. It had happened so often.

When the bloodlust consumes you there is no thought, only action, and when you emerge from your madness it takes a moment to even recall where you are, and you never remember all that you had done. For it wasn't you, it's this thing inside. A true monster.

Phage rolled off the woman and lay on her back, her chest heaving. She was purple with bruises. Every part of her was smeared with blood. She looked fucking awesome.

It felt wrong to be admiring the contours of my wife's damaged body when all around us was death, but I accepted it for what it was. Merely me being a man, adrenaline pumping, joyous in battle and victory, about as primeval as you can get. The thrill of being alive, the pride in defeating a powerful enemy, the knowledge that you can do this, you can survive. It opens up something inside. Something base, yet not cruel or dismissive of life, but celebratory. Almost divine.

I knew that was wrong, but that was exactly how I felt. Close to the oneness of the universe.

Wrapped in the Necroverse.

I would never escape.

No Fucking About

Phage, still prone on the floor, began to shiver, then her entire body jumped, as though she'd been hit with an electric shock. I scrambled over as she convulsed violently. She'd done too much, pushed herself too far, and now she was paying the price. But she'd beat the woman, and she was alive.

I cradled her head and stroked knotted hair while I talked quietly about home. Foam dripped from the corner of her mouth; I wiped it away. Gradually, the fit eased and she came back to herself.

"Hey, how you doing?"

"I hurt like hell but I'll be fine. Did we win?"

"We killed the wardens, we have yet to get to the main course." I smiled weakly; this was not good news.

"They were hard work. Harder than most I've killed. Ugh, that took so much out of me."

"Yeah, me too. I'm wiped out. But this isn't over. You going to be okay?"

"I'll be fine. I just need food and some clean clothes. Preferably warm ones. And will you stop looking at me like that? You dirty old man." Phage's eyes sparkled; she'd be fine.

"Like what? I don't know what you mean?"

"Like you want to roger me right here, right now. Haha, can you imagine?"

I could imagine it for sure. "No, haha, that would be weird. Um, right?"

"Yes, it would. Damn, you do look hot though."

We both felt it, and then some, but even we knew that was a line you didn't cross. Cavorting amongst the corpses of your vanquished foes was a bit too primal, even for us. Plus, we were getting vibes, and it was beginning to get uncomfortable.

I turned to Rocky. He was motionless, sitting with his head lowered, watching from sad eyes.

"How are you doing?" I asked.

"You killed them. I never thought you could do it. I am almost free. Thank you." He turned to look at the still-closed door. What waited for us behind it?

"You did so well," said Phage. "Fought their whispers. Held back as long as you could. Thank you."

"I did as they commanded though. I am ashamed."

"Don't be," Phage told him as she sat up and I did not look at her breasts at all. Why would I?

"I am sorry."

"Rocky, you did great. They were strong practitioners. You defied them, even after all you've been through. That was impressive." I turned to Phage. "Come on, let's get you dressed," I told her, then retrieved her pack so she could find new clothes. The ones she had been wearing were nothing but rags.

"I should have used our special mouse," she said. "Maybe she could have helped us."

"Shh, don't say it aloud." I nodded at the door. Who was behind it?

"And I guess it's for the best. She needs to stay safe." Phage pulled on black jeans, a t-shirt, then a jumper, and shrugged into the coat she'd discarded before her changes. She slipped on her boots and then shouldered her pack. I retrieved mine and did the same. We were here now, and there was no point delaying the inevitable, but then I thought of something and took my pack back off.

"Here, take some more. I'm going to. I think it worked. And it certainly helped you understand Rocky."

Phage took the small shard of crystal I offered and I took another. We crumbled it then stuffed it into our mouths. God, it tasted awful when dry.

I quickly washed it down with water and handed Phage the bottle. She grimaced as she swallowed, but it wasn't going to hurt and might help. My morphing had certainly been easier, and the after-effects less severe, so this was definitely worth keeping as a backup.

Phage's stomach rumbled loudly and I realized just how hungry and weak I felt too. After this amount of action, a sleep was in order, and a massive meal, then plenty of time to recover. We could do none of that if we valued our lives. I grabbed all the provisions I'd brought as emergency rations and we devoured protein-packed bars Phage made most weeks and then stuffed in mouthfuls of dried fruit to give a rapid energy boost.

Rocky sat and watched us the whole time, saying nothing, doing nothing.

Phage began to whisper, calling on her training to repair the superficial wounds and ease our aches and pains. Slowly, we both calmed, the adrenaline eased, and our bodies healed somewhat. It made everything worse, as I was me again, and every bruise and cut throbbed until her magic worked and I could move without pain. We had no permanent damage, so there was no reason to retreat, and even if we could, it would just make matters worse. This had to be done. This had to be finished.

I went and knocked on the door.

"Avon calling," I sang.

"What's Avon?" whispered Phage.

"You know, the make-up people. Aren't they still around?"

"Never heard of them. Is this an old man thing?"

I turned. "What? No. It was just the other year, wasn't it? Okay, maybe before you were born. Anyway, where was I?"

"You were being a twat and knocking on the door."

"Ah, yes." I rapped on the oak. "Hello, any dangerous Necros inside? We've killed your acolytes. Would you like us to kill you too?"

A key rattled in the lock and the door handle turned. We exchanged a glance then both shrugged and with Rocky moving away, terrified, we entered the room.

"I knew you'd make it this far. I knew it!" A man wearing a plain black suit of decent quality once upon a year, clapped his hands in glee, his red face beaming. He was hairless. His bald pate shone orange, reflecting the flames of a freshly lit fire. His teeth were filed into points and horn implants poked from his temples. His nose was gone. Just two vertical slits like a skull's.

It had been all the rage in certain magical circles for a long time now, and had spilled over into alternative fashion amongst many. With medical procedures common for decades, it was still a booming industry. When so much had been taken from us, it was no surprise the disenfranchised youth took it upon themselves to do whatever they could to differentiate themselves, to feel like they belonged to something. To show their defiance.

But this guy was not young, he was not disenfranchised, marginalized, or poor. He was a dark arts practitioner just like Rocky had said. You could read it in his facial tics. The madness in his eyes, the jittery movements, his stooped stance. His body was stripped of every ounce of fat—he burned up all reserves delving deep into places he should run terrified from.

"Look. Behold." He waved his arms as he whispered. The reality of the room screamed as the air tore apart and a rip in the fabric of the universe grew until it reached below the floor and above the ceiling.

First blackness, then an unseen light source highlighted untold sheets of paper. The notes. Dancing and fighting, slapping and caressing each other as they spun in a vortex. Spiraling upwards as old-fashioned calligraphy pens scratched ink onto their surface, giving locations, naming names, never-ending. The sound was incredible, like standing in the middle of a murmuration of starlings numbering in the tens of thousands.

I shrugged, and told him, "Seen it all before. So what?"

The scene faded to black and the rend in our world vanished, leaving the room deathly silent.

"I am so close. I am almost there. Soon I will tear through the final veil and truly discover the truth of the notes."

"And then what?" asked Phage.

"Then I will know, and be able to converse with our masters."

"They don't want you to. Why'd you think we're here?"

"A test, nothing more." He dismissed it; of no import.

"You think so? You are one dumb motherfucker, you know that? And your teeth look stupid. Bet it's a nightmare to brush. Although," I mused, "I guess flossing will be easy. What about apples? How'd you cope with them?"

"What? No, no, stop this. Behold, I will show you the truth of the Necroverse."

He began to whisper, but they were no whispers I'd ever heard before. They weren't threatening; there was no sense of this being directed at us. This man was looking for allies, for acolytes, for replacements to those we'd killed. He was heartless, cruel, but so obsessed with his research and travel into the Necroverse that I honestly don't think he was quite present on this plane.

His whispers spun around the room, thickening and coalescing, calling forth daemons from outside our sphere of reality.

Three huge red beasts coalesced amidst a funk of black smoke this sort loved to use for effect. They glared at us then turned to face their summoner.

"What is it you wish of us?" asked the biggest and baddest.

"I wish to be told of your masters. Show these fools I know the truth of the Necronotes."

"As you wish."

The three daemons turned to us. Without warning, the large window overlooking the gardens on the south side shattered and Tyr slammed into the man, sending him crashing to the floor and into a priceless sideboard. A vase toppled and crashed to the polished golden floorboards.

The daemons vanished.

"Don't you dare kill—"

"Tyr so cold and hungry. But must save Soph and Phage." He looked at me forlornly, then before either of us could act he simply snapped down onto the guy's skull and crushed the bone. As the body slumped sideways, Tyr's eyes became red orbs and he took one quick glance at me before his head shot out and clamped onto the man's throat.

He sucked blood like thick milkshake through a straw until his stomach distended and the man's bowels gave out.

I didn't know whether to be furious or relieved.

"Tyr, what did you do? We could have dealt with him," shouted Phage, but I wasn't so sure.

She moved forward towards Tyr, but I put a hand out to stop her.

"No, keep away. This is going to be extreme. It's his third human, his second Necro, and this guy is, was, seriously powerful. Just stay back, okay? I mean right back."

I guided Phage to the doorway where we held hands and waited with baited breath. Both of us were shaking. We had almost been given information that would have sealed our fates, and all we'd done was stand there and wait for it to happen.

There was no denying it. Tyr had saved not only our lives but the lives of our entire family. Jen, Peth, who knew how many others?

But at what cost to himself?

At what cost to us?

And at what cost to Jen?

Tyr began to change once more.

As he stumbled from the body, his thick neck muscles whipped his head around to face us. His eyes were almost black. Two deep pools of desire. He craved the blood. He needed the blood. Tyrant of the Sky would have the blood.

"It's us, Tyr. Remember?" soothed Phage.

Tyr stared at us, unknowing, but he stilled, then blinked several times. His eyes changed to red, then faded to the familiar strange orange and purple I knew so well.

"Tyr disobeyed. Tyr sorry, but had to save Soph and Phage. Mustn't know the Necronotes. It is forbidden!" he hissed.

"You did save us," I told him. "You should have obeyed, you shouldn't have killed, but I understand why. You had to protect us. But Tyr, it's too soon for you. You will be different forever."

"Tyr knows. Tyr will be strong. Be many things now. Be wizard and see the truth of the notes maybe, whisper and be another man if he wants. Jen can choose. Pick a man and be with Tyr."

"That will never happen. You are a dragon. She is a girl. You can be friends, nothing more."

"Marriage means best friends," said Tyr, not understanding more than that. Too young to know of sex and intimacy, to differentiate between friends and lovers.

"Don't think of that now. Relax, let the change happen. If you fight it, it will be worse. And look, we have a new friend."

Rocky pushed between our legs and sat before Tyr, seemingly unafraid. "Hello. I'm Rocky."

"I am Tyrant of the Sky. He was your master. A bad person. I killed him," he said, too much pride in his words.

"You are my friend." Rocky bowed his head in thanks.

"Be friends with Tyr?" The dragon cocked his head to the side in a very human-like gesture.

"Yes. Friends."

And then Tyr dropped to the floor as the change brought on by human flesh, and blood of the Necroverse, began to irrevocably pull him from his youth and into something that truly was the stuff of nightmares.

It began at the very tip of his tail. The point lengthened, became almost scorpion-like in its sharpness. I wondered if it now actually held a sting. The rest of the tail spasmed, the spastic convulsions lapped up his body like ripples on a still pool as the tail fattened and doubled in length. Soon, his torso was twice as wide but three times as long as before even as the dragon fat of his short youth was burned away. His entire body stretched out to become sleek and much more aerodynamic. The hindquarters were thick with bunched muscle, the rope-like veins pulsing with poisonous, alien blood. Tyr's claws gouged the floorboards and several splintered under his grip as he screamed.

His neck shot forward as his mouth opened wide and I feared we'd be cooked alive, but he dashed to the broken window and let forth an almighty belch of flame that would have burned the entire room to a crisp. Several smaller flames followed, then he once again collapsed and lay there, whimpering, as snow blew in and sizzled before it was even close to our fierce, piping-hot dragon. The air all around him vibrated as heat emanated from this new, utterly deadly creature. His body was burning up as it made the change, stoking the fire within, acid bubbling away with renewed vigor.

Tyr howled in pain as his head cracked. The fused plates of his skull must have separated to accommodate the increased brain size, and I watched the horns sweep back majestically far down his long neck as his teeth fell out and new ones sprang forth three times the size and sharp as a freshly honed knife.

Scales rippled as they thickened, making his hide, and even his once-delicate underbelly harder than any armor known to man. He was a true immortal creature now. You could not blow him up, pierce his body, break his bones, or even snap his claws. Tyr was powerful beyond compare and yet had endless years ahead of him in which to grow even more invulnerable, more fearsome, more deadly, until one day he would be unrecognizable.

The ridges along his back swayed as if in a breeze, and then the strangest thing happened. As they sharpened and bristled to an erect position, so those at the base of his neck dropped off and shattered on the floor.

The gap maybe three feet long flattened out and widened, almost like a saddle. Damn, it was a saddle. One of living flesh. The ridges directly behind the seat blunted and thickened then became part of his hide. The sharpness was gone, replaced with scales. The single ridge in front of the saddle split in two before both protrusions spread slightly apart then angled a few degrees. These too blunted, were rapidly covered in scales. They were handles. And then with a final heave of his body, a deep shudder that shook the floor and caused the chandelier high above to tinkle as it swayed, Tyr bellowed with a pain I could not imagine before his head smashed to the floor, his eyes closed, and he snorted deeply then was still.

The wyrmling, the innocent creature I had spent so much time with on countless occasions, was now long gone. In just a few short years he had become a true creature of the Necroverse.

I had done this to him. My own idiocy for allowing him to accompany me when he should have rested. But that was not his nature. He didn't want to rest. Tyr wanted to fight and hunt and grow and feast like a dragon should. Maybe I wasn't so wrong to allow this, maybe it was exactly what was right and I should have known better than to expect otherwise.

But I pined the loss of the funny little wyrmling, his silly sayings and juvenile antics. He'd been so sweet and comical for years, now that was gone. He grew too fast. I lost a plaything. In its stead I had a true ally, and my entire family had protection from those who would do us harm.

As long as he remembered he was part of our family.

I sat on a rug, and with shaking fingers stuffed my pipe then lit it. As the harsh hit burned my lungs, I could do nothing but stare at the dead man in the room, his head half-missing, and ponder what he'd been about to show us.

"Soph, we have to go."

"Huh?" I turned as Phage shook my shoulder. She was sitting beside me, looking dazzling in a bruised, exhausted, haunted kind of way. I just felt numb. Numbed by the killing, numbed by almost knowing what the truth was, and numbed by my own inability to keep a proper hold on this world. Everything was spiraling out of control. Murders next door. Hit and run drivers. My daughter nearly dying. My wife killing people at my side. Brutalized tigers. And now Tyr and his desire to marry my eleven-year-old. Not to mention the notes and how close we were to maybe understanding their origin.

Did he really know? Had he actually found a way through to the lair of the senders? What if he had? I might learn who they were, but that didn't mean I could stop them. Nobody could.

Around and around in these damn circles of regret and punishment. Question after question. I was sick of the whole fucking thing.

"Soph, it's time to leave."

"Sorry. You okay? Phew, that was a bit hairy. Damn, Tyr's gigantic."

"I know. Look at the size of his teeth." Phage walked a little closer then called for him to wake up. Tyr opened an eye and heaved his monstrous frame up. He collapsed back down, limbs spread-eagled.

"Come on, you great lump," I called as I got up with some help from a handy sideboard. "Time to go home."

"Tyr must rest. Too cold outside."

"You can rest when we're home. We can't stay. This place will be swarming with drones any minute now. You know they make you feel funny and you send them into meltdown. Up."

Tyr struggled to his feet then swung his head around and took in the room. He padded across the floor and hopped up onto the stone window sill then promptly fell back off.

"Take it easy. You have to get used to the new size."

"Feel like the big bus now," he said lazily.

"Good, because you look like one. Fucking beast mode."

Tyr tried again. He crouched, then leaped onto the sill. Claws clung tight to the frame, his hindquarters gripped the sill. He was almost as wide as the window. His tail hung down and along the floor like a fat python after a hearty meal.

"See you at camp," I called, as he dove out of the window then spread his wings once clear.

We turned and left. Rocky followed along, silent and confused.

A Swarm

The peacock called shrilly in the courtyard. I found a tail feather and stuck it into my pack. Jen would like it. It was pretty.

Necrodrones swarmed overhead. Several darted inside the building, more circled the tower, peering through the smashed window. I'd never seen so many in one place. But then, it had been quite a show. Above us they amassed, over a dozen, spinning and circling. Several descended to eye-level and stared right at us with their red, unblinking eyes.

Rocky whined. He didn't like the buzzing.

Neither did I.

Phage and I stood there, shivering, half-starved, almost on our knees, but we held our backs straight, our chins up, and glared, defiant, right back at the Necrobastards.

The damn shame of it all was that our refusal to be beaten, and our proud stature, was probably going down a storm with our unseen masters. Was this why they put us through this? If we'd pissed our pants and tried to hide, would they have upped and moved on to new Necros? Would there be cheers from stadium-sized crowds as they marveled at us staring right back at them? Would there be gasps as Tyr flew off, now larger than a horse? Would there be groans and people hiding their eyes when the cameras zoomed in on the man with half his head missing? And would Rocky's sorry state bring a tear to the eye?

And yet they knew all this was happening. Had watched Rocky be beaten and abused. Allowed the dead Necro to get close to discovering their identity, if he was to be believed. They let us almost die, offered no assistance or encouragement, only hardship.

It was just a game.

I laughed at the drone that came right up close to my face. I grinned and I guffawed like a clown. My face was battered and bruised, I might have broken my nose somehow, for probably the fiftieth time at least, and I wasn't sure, but I was wondering if I had actually swallowed a bit of an ear.

Phage laughed with me. Husband and wife, in the snow, bloodied yet unbowed, laughed at the Necroverse.

The drones shot up then vanished.

No doubt the bodies were gone, all signs of our fight eradicated. I wondered what would happen to the place now there was nobody here to guard it. What about the volunteers? How would that be explained away? It wouldn't. They'd vanished. There would be no trace. We had to leave. I suspected that within hours, maybe a day, more volunteers would arrive to replace the missing, and new security installed to safeguard an important piece of British heritage.

After all, the draconian lockdown measures had to end sometime, and maybe then the castle would once again throng with the laughter of children and the warm smiles of elderly couples walking hand in hand, admiring the beauty of the well-tended borders. Until then, it was just a dead monument to a long-forgotten past.

Forgotten by most, but I was here when the castle was built. I helped build the bloody thing, after all. The south tower was mine. I laid the stones, ran the crew, worked all hours in an effort to forget what haunted my dreams and took me away from an honest day's work for a few days every year while I murdered for no reason I could possibly fathom.

Still couldn't. I was no wiser. Just more jaded by it all.

But it was nice that I'd been a part of this, and at least the bloody Necrodrones hadn't simply blasted it out of existence. That would have been a real shame.

I took Phage's hand, and with a nod to Rocky we left the castle and headed down the winding road back towards camp. The going was tough, we constantly slipped, one helping the other up. Neither of us could walk properly as the drain was immense after so much shifting and morphing. Controlling the animals had been the final straw for my limited gifts.

I couldn't really even imagine what Phage felt like. She was shivering uncontrollably now, and her teeth chattered. I removed my jacket and wrapped her up as best I could, rammed an extra woolly hat on her head and moved us as fast as I could.

We made it back to camp eventually, where there was a nice surprise waiting for us.

"Bernard, you made a bonfire!"

"I thought you'd be cold. And I'm freezing." He shook dramatically, the daft lump. I didn't argue with him about never experiencing extremes of temperature. I simply couldn't be arsed.

"Thank you, my friend. I assume you know what happened?"

"I'm a unicorn," was his reply.

"Yes, you are. This is Rocky. He's coming home with us. He's our new friend."

"Hello Rocky."

"Hello. Bernard, was it?"

"Yes, Bernard. I like your stripes. Very... er... stripy."

"And I like your... um... horn! Yes, your horn. It's... er... very horny."

There was a moment of awkward silence, then every one of us burst out laughing. It was that or weep for our sins.

"Where's Tyr? He killed, and he fed on a powerful Necro. He's as big as you now, Bernard. Well, almost."

"He's there, in the fire. I think he's asleep."

I peered into the huge fire that Bernard had somehow managed to stack into a perfect pyramid. If I squinted, I could almost make out the form of Tyr curled up as tight as he could into a ball with his tail over his head. He was basically invisible.

"Guess we should let him sleep then." I turned to Phage. "How are you doing?"

"Exhausted. Let's eat. Can you make tea?"

"Sure. No problem." I sorted out the kettle to boil then gathered all the food we'd brought with us and we tucked in, eating pasta salad, strips of cooked meat, boiled eggs, fruit, and biscuits by the bag full. I fried up chicken, reveling in the smoke stinging my eyes and the harsh tang as I inhaled. It meant I was alive. We washed it all down with several cups of sugar-laden tea. Or whatever it was they used nowadays instead of sugar.

Rocky ate a little, but seemed so relieved to be away from the castle that he couldn't keep his eyes open.

After an hour of steady eating and the fire blazing, with the animals all asleep and the day coming to a close, I finally felt at least partially normal. Not *normal* normal, but I wasn't wounded too badly, my nose had healed a little thanks to Phage's weak whispers, and everything else would sort itself out in time.

Phage was merely bruised physically, with several small cuts but nothing to worry about. It was her energy levels that were the problem. She was still shivering, and was losing weight before my eyes. The multiplying of her form certainly drained her, but it was the change into the beast that really made her suffer. All that size and strength, it had to come from somewhere. It came from both the Necroverse and from within. And the harder she used that form, the more risk she took.

She'd live, but I had to get her fed more, and get her home. It would have to wait until the morning. There was no way we could travel in the dark, not even with Bernard's gifts.

I wrapped Phage up with blankets and then collected as much firewood as I could find before darkness fell.

Back at camp, with Phage sitting on a log as close to the fire as she dared, I prodded the sleeping dragon and finally woke him up. Tyr stretched out amid the flames, looking like a devilish phoenix, and yawned happily.

"Tyr is warm. Tyr is mighty warrior. Tyr feels good."

"Yeah, I bet you do. Now scoot. I want you out of there so I can use the space you took up to add this wood."

Tyr reluctantly exited the flames. Sparks flew high into the darkening sky as he settled himself beside the fire with his tail trailing into the flames. It would have to do.

I busied myself with physical work, taking care to lay out the logs and broken branches in a way that would keep the fire going for the night. Large stump at the edge away from us, the logs resting on it so they would slowly burn and dry it out.

All set, I rummaged around for more food then insisted Phage eat as much as she possibly could. She ate, and ate, and ate until finally she began to come back to herself. Her cheeks reddened, she smiled, and there she was. My beautiful wife.

"Hey, welcome back to the land of the living."

"Thanks. It's good to be here. Wow, I was so zonked. Haven't felt like that for years."

"You fought hard. And part of it's the stress. Nothing like working with your husband to raise the cortisol."

"It wasn't as bad as I expected it to be. I thought I'd freeze. I didn't want you to see me doing those things."

"I felt the same. We did good. Now it's over."

"Yes. It's over."

Phage stared into the fire for the longest time. I watched Tyr as his chest rose and fell. What were we going to do with him now? Eleven, but already the size of a dragon twice his age. And that saddle on his back. He was gearing up to allow Jen to ride him. His body knew what to do even if his head didn't. He was so keen to be with her that it had made the change far sooner than was customary.

Such was the power of the dragon mind and its connection to the Necroverse. He knew what he wanted and I don't know that any of us were in a position to stop him now. I must remain strong, assert my position, ensure he knew who was in charge and what was expected of him. I didn't even want to contemplate what would happen otherwise.

I considered taking Phage into the castle, but figured we were probably warmer here with the fire than in a freezing building with a small blaze in a hearth. And besides, I thought it best to stay away from the place. Who knew what was going on in there? Could have been anything. The sky was clear, no signs of snow, so curling up beside the fire seemed the best bet.

I smoked my pipe and watched the flames tickle the air. Night hurried to fill the void left by the low sun, and it wasn't long before we were marooned on an island of light when all around was pitch.

As the creatures slept, I nudged Phage when the sprites came to visit. They were cautious at first, same as always, but once they felt safe they began to play. They circled, they spun, they dove, they danced. They sang songs we had no way of understanding and we didn't need to. Being a part of their display was reward enough.

Phage was transfixed, her smile beautiful.

"I've never seen them before," she whispered. "Does this happen often?"

"There's never any way to tell. They can be absent for years, decades, then they find me and come out to celebrate our reunion. The older you get, the more you'll see them. You're still a youngster. Sometimes I feel like I'm too old for you, that I shouldn't have taken you when I did."

"Nonsense. Soph, look at me." I turned and stared into the eyes of the woman I loved more than I had any other. "You saved me. You took me from Mother and her madness and you saved me. I know we joke about the kidnapping, but it was what I wanted. What I wanted since I first set eyes on you. Do you remember that?"

I nodded. "I remember. You dropped something, so I rushed over to help you. The gentlemanly thing to do."

"Yes, a book. When I saw you then, I knew. I said to myself that I would marry you. That you would be a fine husband and a great father. I wasn't wrong."

"And when I saw you I thought the same thing. Haha, you know what I mean." We kissed. Slow, tender, full of love. A deep connection, the truth of our closeness in the simple act of lips touching. More said than in a thousand words.

"Mother hated you." Phage's eyes twinkled.

"I know. Still does."

"No, not any more. She trusts you. She admires you. But she doesn't like that you talk back to her. Nobody does that."

"Yeah, well, I can't help it. You two okay? You had a bit of a run-in before we left."

"Just the usual. You know how she is. Always wanting to push things."

"We're talking about Jen, right?"

"Yes. Mother wants to train her, like she did me. I told her again, absolutely not. But you know what she's like."

"Pushy. Always wants her own way. Won't take no for an answer. Always thinks she's right."

"Yes. Gosh, have I turned into my mother?"

"No, but I think I might have. Haha, what a family."

"We don't do too badly, considering."

"We do bloody great, considering. I mean, look at us. In the middle of nowhere, outside in the snow, killing people, surrounded by talking animals. Unicorns, dragons, tigers, you don't get that for Christmas unless you live our kind of life."

"No. Imagine if none of it happened. If it was just the three of us living on a quiet farm and there was no craziness."

"Honestly? I can't imagine that. I don't know what that would be like. How others live that way."

"It's not the life for us," she agreed. "We weren't brought up that way. We don't know that life. All the other parents, when I talk to them, it doesn't seem real. It's like it's make-believe, that they know nothing about our world."

"I know what you mean. It's too different. Too far removed from this Necro life. We have each other, that's the main thing. So get used to it. We're going to be around for a long time."

Phage squeezed my hand. "Forever, I hope."

"Me too. More than anything."

Constable Again

"Hello?"

"Fuck, who's that?" I jumped up, knife unclipped, ready for whatever this was.

A man emerged from the trees with his hands up. I recognized him. I didn't exactly relax, but I was relieved I didn't have to fight.

Rocky growled. Tyr opened an eye then closed it again. Bernard continued to snore.

"It's okay, Rocky. Go back to sleep. He means us no harm." Rocky, trusting me, returned to his happy slumber. The poor thing had probably never felt so safe in his entire life.

"May I approach?" asked the Constable.

"Do we have a choice?" I asked gruffly.

"There is always a choice, Necrosoph."

I smarted at the use of my full name. "Come on over and join the party."

The Constable, a man who'd come to our house four years ago, walked slowly into the light. He was dressed in a faded, nondescript black suit, a fedora, a heavy overcoat dusted with snow, and a black scarf wrapped tight around his neck. His black leather gloves were good quality, but he still wore the same shoes as before—hardly ideal for the conditions.

"How'd you get here?" I asked.

"I was brought," he said, eyes already boring into my head, trying to read me. Not trying. He was. His stare was as focused as Tyr's, but much more scary. A word from a man like this could mean the end of all you held dear. He knew I knew that, but he would also know I wouldn't let it make me weak.

"Fair enough. Not usual though, is it? Especially in this weather?"

"I do as I am asked." He sounded pissed off but was trying to hide it. Or maybe that was just me projecting. Or him trying to make us feel more comfortable. This was why I hated Constables—you never knew what they were up to.

"We haven't done anything wrong," said Phage. "Do you want tea?"

"Oh, tea would be a delight! Thank you. And I apologize for the imposition. But you understand?"

"We do," replied Phage kindly.

The man had to do his job. He'd been chosen specifically to be a Constable, and had undergone years of training to read people like he could see the future, know the past. In a way he could. Think of a seer, a sorcerer, a dragon's insights, someone who could tap into the Necroverse and predict all possible outcomes. That was a Constable. A Bene Gesserit made real. Most hated the job. None had a choice.

"You had a busy day," noted the Constable as he took his tea and nodded thanks to Phage.

"We did. Did you see?" I was fishing, wondering if he'd give us an insight.

"I do my job," was his cryptic reply.

We watched and waited. What were we supposed to say?

"Now, I have a few questions if you don't mind?"

"And if we do?" I asked.

"You know how this works, I'm sure." He sounded weary, like he really didn't want to be here. But then, who would? I know I didn't.

"We do."

"After the two women in the ballroom were killed, what happened?"

"Oh, so that's what it was," said Phage.

"Yes, they would hold balls, have parties, that kind of thing, in long halls. It was a beautiful sight."

He spoke wistfully, as though he'd been there, done that, got the funny hat to prove it. I never got invited. I was the builder, not the aristocracy.

"We played it by the book," I told him. "We went into the room, the man showed us the notes being made, said he could get to the ones responsible for the notes. He called some daemons. They were going to tell us. He had a hold over them. Then Tyr came and ate his face off. The end."

"And the daemons? What did they say?"

"They just said they would do what the man said," Phage told him. "But they didn't get a chance to tell us anything. Like Soph said, Tyr put an end to that."

"Ah, yes, the dragon." We all turned to watch Tyr sleeping. He flickered in and out of view as he dreamt his dragon dreams.

"He's a growing lad," I noted.

"Indeed. Now, Phage, do you know why you were both assigned the Necronote?" He focused intently on her as he spoke, reading every movement, every shifting of the eyes, every twitch of the mouth.

"No. Of course not. I mean, we wondered, of course we did. But do I know for a fact? No."

"Why do you think you were both sent?"

"As a test of some sort? Because he was a powerful man and he had acolytes. Because they wanted a good show?" Phage shrugged.

"Soph? What about you? Do you believe there is a reason you and your wife were sent together?"

"Yes, I do. It's to see how we work together. And to see what we tell each other. How much we would discuss when under high pressure, and what we might say once it was over. If we lived."

"And what did you tell each other?"

"That we want to go home," said Phage.

"And that we wish we didn't have to do it. That we want it to stop and never have to kill again. But they know that, don't they? They know what happened."

"Not all. That is why I am here. There is only so much the drones see. Only so much that can be gleaned from the eyes."

"The eyes?"

"The tears in the fabric of our reality. The rips. The splitting apart of our world and the access to another place. They are called eyes. You have seen them. Glimpses when you see the notes created, or how bodies are sometimes disposed of. They are the eyes."

"Oh, I see," said Phage. "We saw the notes, we saw the daemons, we saw nothing else. What have you seen?"

"I have seen much, but not all. Nobody sees all. Nobody knows. But I have said too much. Thank you for your time. And thank you for the tea. Most delicious, and truly welcome on such a night." He nodded, then placed his mug down on the ground. The Constable put on his hat, adjusted it, then pulled on the nice gloves and rose. With a weak smile, he walked off towards the castle.

"That was weird," said Phage.

"Was it? Weirder than everything else?"

"No, I guess not."

We huddled close together, and wondered once again what the Constable's report might contain.

I thought I heard the distant sound of a helicopter, but I could have been mistaken.

We said nothing. What was there to say? I don't think anything could have shocked us this night. We'd done about all there was to do.

Phage's phone rang, muffled by the layers of protection.

She fumbled inside her coat until she found it, then removed it from the case. "Hello?

"...Yes, it's me, Mother. What is it?..."

"...What do you mean in the garden?..."

"...Yes, of course I know what the garden is. Don't speak to me like that..."

"...I'm sorry too..." Phage listened for a moment, her eyes going wide. "...Just standing there?..."

"What's wrong?" I asked.

Phage waved me silent then asked, "Is Jen okay?..." She waited for the reply. "...Good. Can you keep it that way? Don't do anything, we'll be there soon..."

"...We will. God, will this never end?..."

"...Yes, bye."

"We have to go, and I mean now." Phage was panicked, already grabbing gear and loading her pack.

"What happened? Jen's okay?"

"Jen's fine. They're both in the house. But there are people in the garden."

"What people? Why is Peth so worried?"

"Because they're calling, and they're about to do something."

"Do what? What people? Phage, you're scaring me. Fuck, what's happening."

"In a moment, okay? Tyr, Bernard, Rocky, everyone wake up. Now! I said now!"

The animals stirred from their slumber and got to their feet, then waited for Phage to speak.

"Everyone, and sorry to tell you like this, Soph, but we have to be quick. Back at home," Phage took a deep breath and tried to compose herself, but I could see she was close to the edge, "there are a group of Necros in the garden. They're calling for you, Tyr. They want you. Soph, they said they knew you. Peth heard them say they wanted to kill you and take the dragon."

"Who are they?"

"Mother doesn't know. But Jen is inside the house and she is scared. We must go. And I mean right away. Bernard, can you carry both of us on your back?"

"I could if I had to," he said morosely.

"Then you have to. Tyr, under no circumstances are you to show yourself until we arrive, and only once we give an order. Is that clear?"

"Tyr understands. Why men want Tyr?"

"Because you're a dragon," I told him.

"Tyr is mighty warrior," he agreed.

"Rocky, um, you don't know the way. I'm not sure what to do."

"I do. Tyr, you're huge now, can you carry Rocky back home? How fast can you fly? How long will it take you?"

"No time at all. Tyr can morph now. Fed on man in castle. Got lots of powers. Want to see?"

"Later, okay? Right, so grab Rocky and get back there, but both of you, remain hidden. Do you understand? This is beyond important."

"Tyr understand."

"I understand," said Rocky.

"I can't hear them anymore," said Phage. "The crystal must have worn off."

I pulled it out and said, "Here, take a large piece. This isn't the time to not be able to understand them."

Phage nodded and chewed on dried shards as I handed her some water and she gulped from the flask.

"Should we morph?" I wondered.

"I don't even know if I can now. And even if we made it that far, what state would we be in? No, Bernard can get us there very fast, can't you?"

"I will do my best."

"Okay, let me get my things," I said. I grabbed all I thought I would need, stuffed it into my pack, and then we climbed onto Bernard. Me in front, Phage with her arms wrapped around my waist.

"Tyr, don't forget, stay hidden. We'll speak once we arrive. Do not kill anyone or burn anything unless we give the okay. This is important. Bernard, you ready?"

"Go like the wind, Bernard," said Phage, then she coughed as the dry crystal moved into her system.

"Let's go."

Bernard turned, trotted out of the forest, then wasted no time picking up speed until in seconds we were supersonic.

There were no dreams of candyfloss and bonbons. My head was too panicked, my heart too close to breaking, my soul too weary. I had visions of dead daughters and the earth exploding in nuclear Armageddon instead. For the first time, I didn't feel happy riding a unicorn going faster than the speed of sound.

Twats with Hats

It took ten minutes to arrive home. Bernard could get a serious move on if he wanted to. Of course, he'd blown it for the future, because now we knew exactly what he was capable of. He didn't even take us to the wrong address.

We jumped down, stressed and exhausted, but the adrenaline was rising and with it our ability to commit the most violent of acts. Phage ran to the house and knocked on the door, calling for Peth, while I marched around to the rear. The bright light that lit up the garden was on, and so were the lights for the zoo and the outbuildings. Peth clearly wanted to see what the intruders were up to.

"Haha, try it again," said a man I recognized.

One of four other guys with him nodded, adjusted his hat, then swung a thick branch at the troll statue. Obviously, the branch snapped.

"Ow, haha, felt that right up my arm. Damn, what's this thing made of?"

"Rock, you fucking moron," I told him as I walked towards them down the slushy lawn.

"Ah, here he is, the man himself. Sys, this is that fucker from the other month. The one that nearly snapped my neck when I just wanted to have a chat."

"I told you then, and I'll tell you now, I don't want to talk. Now fuck off."

"And I'm telling you, you don't treat a guy like that. You made me look bad, and I ain't standing for it. Time to pay for it, old man." He pulled off his woolen hat and stuffed it into a pocket. I'm sure he felt it held significance, but for me all it meant was he'd have a cold head.

"Look, Pete, wasn't it?"

"Yeah, that's me." He grinned, and cracked his knuckles. It might have impressed his buddies, a bunch of dickheads with only a brain cell between them and a damaged one at that, but it didn't impress me.

"Pete, that was between us. If you want to fight it out, fine, although I am knackered. But what, you come here, to my home, *my fucking home!*" I roared, "and bring four guys with you? You too much of a coward to face me on your own? And it took you this long to build up the courage, did it?"

"Nah, I knew you got the shit kicked out of you and were in the hospital. Figured I'd wait until you got better." Pete spun one of his many piercings, twisting the ball on a hoop at his ear. Then he grinned and ran his hands through his short hair. "But here I am. And I want that dragon."

"So this isn't about your idiot pride at all? You want my dragon and this is your excuse?"

"Hey, figured I'd kill two birds with one stone. And one of those birds is you, haha. Get it?"

"Man, you are so fucking dumb. I can't believe you're still alive. What are you, kid? In your late twenties?"

"Twenty-nine. What of it?"

"Look, all of you, you don't have to do this. You have your whole lives ahead of you, if you don't get killed next note, which is very likely considering the idiot things you clearly get involved in, but I don't want to fight you. Not even you, Pete. I want a quiet life, to be left alone. I have killed more people than your ages combined. Do you understand what I'm saying?"

Pete and his cronies tried to do the math but clearly weren't up to it. I sighed.

"I'm three hundred and forty-four. That means I've killed a minimum of a man a year for over three centuries. Shit, your ages together don't even come to a hundred and fifty. You think five youngsters can get the better of me? You're mistaken."

"Maybe we should go, Pete. He's right. Look at him, he ain't even scared. This ain't worth it."

"Go if you want, you coward," spat Pete. "I'm taking what I want, and I might even take that little wife of yours for a spin too. How'd you like that, old man?"

I kept cool. I didn't shout, or lose the plot. I knew how to handle situations like this.

"Okay, listen up, all of you. Most of you can go if you want." I pointed to the one having second thoughts.

He turned to his buddies, then back to me, and said, "Sorry, this was stupid." He ran off, so we were down to four.

"Now, Pete here just threatened my wife in the worst way imaginable. For that, I will kill him. I absolutely will kill him and there is nothing any of you can do to stop me. Understand? The question you have to ask yourself is if you want to get in my way. If you do, if you so much as say a disparaging word to me now, take too long to think about it, or are still here in ten seconds, then I will assume you too might harm my wife. I have a young daughter and her grandmother in the house, and a lot of animals here. You are scaring them all. I will not have my home desecrated." I turned to Pete. "You should know better than this. You do not come to a man's home. Ever. It's the way."

"What fucking way?" he snarled.

"The way a man should live his life. If you want vengeance, fine. You go about it like a man, with pride and honor. You don't come to his home and threaten his family." I looked from one man to the other. "So, now we all know where we stand. One. Two. Three. Four..."

There was panic in their eyes, apart from Pete and one other man. I studied him carefully and realized he was no youngster. He was old, seasoned. And quiet. Smart, in other words. Letting Pete have all the attention so he could come at me.

"You should all leave. Especially you." I pointed to the older guy. He just stared back blankly.

"Pete, you're going to get yourself and your buddies killed." He smiled again, that cocky grin. He wouldn't back off. He was too dumb for that. He thought he'd beat me. I don't know why. Plain idiocy I guess. Or maybe he had something up his sleeve. Literally.

I glanced at his puffy jacket. He could have a weapon up there that he figured would give him an edge. A gun? Probably.

"Five. Six. Seven. Last chance, guys."

"They're staying, right?" said Pete. "Not like that fucking traitor that ran off. He'll get his later."

The others spread out and nodded that they would stay. They didn't look happy about it and neither was I. Last thing I wanted to do was kill kids. The older man glared at me. He didn't care. This veteran was happy to risk it for the prize they'd come after. If I had to guess, he was the one really behind this, using Pete's dumbness as an excuse to get him to come along.

"Eight. Look, go home. I honestly don't want to hurt you. Would you really throw away the chance to live for centuries? Please, go home. You'll die otherwise."

"Just finish your counting," said the old guy. He pulled out a knife from a sheath and gripped it expertly. He was the one to watch, not Pete the pierced.

"Pete, I'm asking you. Go home. I don't need this, you don't need this. My guess, it was this guy's idea. He doesn't care about you. Your friend just wants the dragon. He couldn't care less about me and you. Please."

"It was my idea! Not Jonas'," he growled. "These are my buddies, my amigos, and they're backing me up. We gonna party or what? And where's the sweet dragon? You've got a lot of other nice creatures down there," he laughed. "We're gonna take them all. Have ourselves a fucking zoo."

"You won't get near them. Okay, I asked nicely. It's your choice, all of you. Nine."

I morphed.

Rule number one in a fight, I reminded myself. Play dirty.

My mantra. My salvation.

I slit the throat of one of the youngsters before he even knew what was happening. I slid past and was on to the next. He was faster, and dodged as I punched out with the knife. His blade came at my face, but he was an amateur and I brushed his arm aside, jabbed him in the kidney with a left, then kneed him in the face as he bent double.

Skirting behind his back, I yanked him by the hair, said, "Sorry," and pulled my arm back to stab him.

Something caught my elbow. The older man. Jonas. He smirked as his knife came expertly at my side, but I morphed and he got nothing but air. Pete roared and charged like a dumb bull, pulling out the gun as he did so. I skidded behind the troll and ducked down as Pete fired round after round.

What an absolute dick. The bullets ricocheted off the huge form and Pete just kept on coming, grinning like he was invulnerable. He didn't even seem concerned when he ran out of bullets.

"Stripe, you still with us, buddy?" I called out mentally to an old friend. He was awake and keen to join the fray, but had held back out of the code so many of us went by.

"I'm here for you."

Within seconds, I spotted the black and white badger bounding up the garden. I smiled at the tubby form of my old friend.

"Haha, look, he's got backup," laughed one of the men as Stripe skidded to a halt in front of the three men while Pete paused to check it out.

"Yeah. Oh no, we're doomed. Haha."

Stripe's bones cracked as his body changed, and he became his true self. A huge, misshapen goblin with long arms thicker than a man's legs and a torso knotted with muscles. Shame about the knees. They looked like he was using the saggy skin to store rocks.

"Which one first?" he asked.

"Take your pick," I called. I dodged left, then right around the troll as Pete lunged to grab me.

Stripe roared as he crouched then dove at the nearest man. He smashed into him, sending him flying, then jumped onto the stupid kid and presumably kicked the shit out of him. I had no time to watch. I had my own fish to attend to.

With Pete deciding to change tack, he stood stock still and scrunched up his face in concentration. He morphed, but it was scrappy and misjudged so he came up far to my left. I was so pissed off with the whole thing that I acted rashly and just stepped up to him and hissed, "Let's play, motherfucker," which was a lame line and a bit macho, but I was tired and he really was annoying.

"Bring it on." He sneered, and widened his stance, moved his knife back and forth from hand to hand. I mean, who does that?

Being an old hand at this kind of thing, I didn't just go for it, I checked on the others. Stripe was pulverizing one guy, the older man was watching, waiting, and I didn't trust him. He was the kind to stab you in the back while you were busy fighting someone else. Just like I would do.

Pete shouted something incomprehensible and then ran at me, keeping low to make a smaller target. I slid forward onto my back and kicked his legs out from under him. He went down hard and I rolled onto him then pinned my knife right through his forearm. He screamed and batted at me but I punched him in the face repeatedly until his nose was mush and his eyes were so swollen he could hardly see.

"I'll kill you," he hissed through broken teeth.

"Not today, Pete. Not ever." I yanked my knife free then reluctantly slit his throat. Blood spurted. Steam rose as the frigid air met the warm juice. Pete lost his battle with life itself and went on to whatever came next.

The base of my neck tingled and I rolled aside as Jonas' knife slashed through the air, narrowly missing me. Spreadeagled as I was, I made an easy mark and he grinned as he booted me in the ribs then immediately drew back to get one at my head. I put my arms up to protect my skull just as the kick connected. It hurt like a bitch but at least my noggin wasn't cracked.

Damn, I was so tired. I honestly did not have the energy for this. No next kick came, so I peeked out to find Phage with the guy in a headlock while he batted ineffectively at her. His knife was on the ground. I kicked it away, scrambled to my feet, and nodded to Phage as I whacked him in the guts. She released him as he doubled over and I sideswiped him. He took it well and careened into my stomach, knocking the wind from me. Phage moved away, presumably to help Stripe if he needed it.

"This was all your idea, right?" I asked breathlessly.

"I want me that dragon. You know what they can do for you?"

"I'm just finding out. But today ain't your birthday, and you get no gift from us," I told him.

"We'll see about—"

I morphed, came up behind Jonas and stuck him in the side twice, jab, jab, but I knew from experience it might not be fatal.

He grunted and spun, smashed me in the face with his elbow, and I staggered backwards, temporarily blinded, unable to remain standing as I slid on the slush and my legs snapped out from under me. I landed hard, the wind gone again, and cursed yet another broken nose.

The world was strangely silent. I couldn't tell why though. Then I understood.

Stripe stood, unmoving, as I got to my feet. Jonas had Phage in front of him, his knife tight to her neck, blood already drawn. The other Necro was a bloody mess but he moved beside him and they stood there, grinning, as Stripe and I moved closer after I gave him the nod.

"Stop right there. That's close enough. You and your freak here."

"You're the freak," I told Jonas. "You hurt her, I will make you suffer for an eternity."

"I don't think so. You got to admit when you're beat. And you, my friend, most definitely are. Me and Silas here are going to take your dragon, take whatever we want, and have ourselves a good time. You are going to watch and you are going to stay right fucking there. Both of you."

"Then you may as well kill her."

"What?"

Phage's eyes widened in surprise, but I held her gaze while I spoke to the man.

"If you are going to rape her, abuse her, and think I'll watch, then I won't. So, like I said, you may as well carry out your threat, because I will not let that happen. Her daughter is inside the house. *My fucking daughter*," I hissed, "and I can only imagine what she would become if she knew what was done to her mother while I stood by. It will not happen."

"Then I guess I'll kill her." Jonas slid the knife expertly across Phage's neck.

It took every ounce of my willpower not to break down and scream into the night. But I remained stoic. Not a flicker of emotion crossed my face as blood ran from the neck of my beloved.

Things Heat Up

"Haha, you are one cold son-of-a-bitch."

Phage remained perfectly still as the Necro kept his knife tight at her throat. The cut wasn't deep enough to kill, just bloody enough to get the message across.

Stripe and I moved towards the statue with a nod from me, but we retained our distance from the others so they wouldn't do anything hasty.

"So, what now? You know if you murder Phage then you're both dead, right?"

"It's looking that way. I've never met a man who wouldn't cave under these circumstances. Who the fuck are you?"

"Me? I'm just a guy with a family. I want peace, not this crap. It's Phage who is the real tough one. Hey Phage. You okay?"

She smiled sadly, not wanting to risk moving her head. She knew I loved her, that what was happening was the only way we might escape with our lives. Her life. That's what was important here.

"No talking," Jonas warned. To get his point across, he cut Phage again.

"Motherfucker." I almost lost it. My head pounded, my vision blurred by the bloodlust, but I continued the act and stood there as casually as I could, doing nothing.

Nothing they could see.

I called out mentally to Bernard and, thankfully, he understood what I was asking. He walked casually into the garden and stopped beside us near the statue then lowered his head as though he were a meek, dumb creature. Only one of those was true.

"See, I told you," said Jonas. "He's got a fucking unicorn too."

"No way. Look at that horn. You know how much a unicorn's horn is worth?" laughed the dumb youngster as he moved beside Bernard.

I shook my head at Bernard as he tensed. He could slaughter the guy with a single, well-placed thrust, but he stood stock still and did as I asked.

"A goddamn fortune! Haha, we're gonna be rich. Millionaires. Okay, call the others. We need them. This is gonna take a while."

Silas took out his phone, made a brief call, and then a half-dozen men appeared from the far end of the land as they bashed their way through the fences and gates, making an almighty racket.

"Backup has arrived."

"Why'd you keep them hidden?" I asked, genuinely interested.

"They were the reserves. In case things got hairy. Never show all your cards in the first hand. Worked out alright, I'd say."

I glanced at the corpses. "You think?"

"Pete was a dumbass, a real crackerjack. These guys, they're the real deal. Hey fellas."

Phage's captor nodded to the six men who spread out across the trampled lawn and did some mighty fine glaring at me and Stripe.

"Hello," I said. "As I was saying to this gentleman, if you would care to leave, that'd be great. If you stay, if you threaten me or my family, or the animals, or ruin my fucking garden any more, then you will all die. Every single one of you. Understand?"

They laughed, and turned to their leader. One asked, "Jonas, is he serious?"

"He's a tough, cold bastard to be sure. Yeah, he's serious. They got two of our guys. The other kid ran off. But I got this here woman for us to have some fun with and there's another one inside, and a kid."

"Sweet. So, who's first? I like to go first."

"Hey, no fair. I wanna go first," said one of the others.

"Nobody does anything until we sort this mess out. We get the dragon, this unicorn, and what else you got down there in your fucking barns?"

"I'll show you if you like," I sneered.

Betty and Kayin came up from the stables, followed by the entire zoo—those who were awake at this time or could be roused. I didn't ask them to act, never forced myself on them, merely told them what was happening and that these men had threatened all of us. Them, and us. That they would be taken and most likely killed or sold if I or Phage were hurt. I also told them all that they had threatened Jen, the young girl that most had known since she was a baby.

"Haha, look at these tiny horses," a man laughed. "They're smaller than my rabbit."

"You got a rabbit?" another asked him.

"Yeah, you got a problem with that?"

"Enough!" shouted Jonas. "Fuck! Three unicorns. We really are gonna be rich."

The men rubbed their hands together greedily, grinning like the fools there were.

Several goats began gnawing at the clothes of the newcomers and they shooed them off. The other animals crowded around, acting dumb but excited, and the men laughed and joked at the various creatures. They marveled at some, made fun of others, petted those they thought cute.

"So, you can talk to them all?" asked Jonas.

"I can."

"No funny business," he warned.

"What's he gonna do," a man called, "make them lick us?"

"No, you idiot. Make them kick the shit out of you." Jonas turned back to me. "I'm warning you. Do not make me finish her."

"Like I told you, and that goes double now. You may as well slaughter us both because you are not going to defile her." I turned to the other men. "My daughter is in there. You think this is right? That you threaten us like this when a young girl is scared and hiding?"

"Go get her," Jonas told one of the older men.

It took every ounce of my self control not to lose myself to the bloodlust, but I stood my ground as the man Jonas had spoken to sauntered past the animals and passed me with a wicked grin.

"You better be who I think you are," I muttered.

The man turned. "What?"

"Nothing. Just talking to him." I pointed.

He turned.

The troll thrust out a fist and very literally smashed the man's head into pulp.

The troll's arm was stationary in the stretched position. He didn't budge an inch. For a moment, all was silent, and then all hell broke loose.

Betty tore into the man nearest her, spiking him directly through the back of the head with a single, perfect thrust that cracked through the guy's skull, out his eye, and into the man directly in front. She lifted them both off the ground and shook wildly, flinging the corpses into a man to the right.

Kayin, eager to get in on her first bit of action, neighed madly then reared up and kicked her hooves into a panicked Necro, tearing off his ear then trampling him as he fell. The guy scrambled to his feet and tried to run, but Bernard dashed forward with his head low and drove his horn through the loser's midsection.

The others panicked, pulled knives and began to advance on poor Kayin, who was by no means ready for such madness. I ordered all the animals back to their quarters and, although reticent, I promised everything would be alright. They stampeded, crushing the dead into the soggy ground as they raced to the comfort and security of their homes. Within the space of several seconds, the entire zoo had left—it would take ages to repair all the fences and gates.

"Now!" I shouted to Phage as Jonas was distracted by the mayhem, unable to decide what to do. Whether to kill Phage or keep her as hostage.

Phage became the beast.

Her clothes ripped, her body expanded, her hide thickened until it was almost as tough as Tyr's. As Jonas realized what was happening, she was already turning. She gripped his knife arm with both meaty, misshapen hands and snapped it like a twig.

Jonas howled, the other man ran at us, and I knew we'd be beaten if I didn't let at least one of the animals be a little more corrupted. No way could I risk the unicorns getting more involved. They shouldn't have to kill, it wasn't their nature, and much as I saw the bloodlust in Kayin, I knew she wasn't up to the fight just yet.

There was only one thing for it. As Jonas pulled a gun with his left hand and aimed at Phage, I shouted loudly, "Okay, Tyr, forget everything I said. I want you to incinerate the fucking lot of them. I want you to destroy as many of these bastards as you possibly can. You have my permission to burn, melt, eat, kill in any way you can. Understand? Kill them all!"

"Tyr will burn," he hissed with dangerous glee. He sighed, an addict given permission to get the biggest fix of his life. What would emerge after so much killing, I had no idea. But when it came to family, I would do whatever it took to ensure they survived. Even risk Tyr's life.

Even as we spoke, darkness filled the sky as the massive form of Tyr sped low. He dropped Rocky beside Jonas then soared away. The tiger growled then tore at his leg, taking a fat chunk of flesh from his thigh. The remaining three men aimed and fired at Tyr in a panic as the Tyrant of the Sky plummeted and swept across the now utterly ruined lawn. Bullets stopped dead when they hit his immortal hide, and with fathomless glee our magnificent dragon belched a geyser of flame that would do any bonfire aficionado proud.

Men ran screaming as their skin blistered and bubbled, their heads human torches.

I ran after Jonas as he limped away, while Phage dropped to her knees and her beautiful naked body rolled in the filthy slush to escape Tyr's madness. He was wild, uncontrollable, spiraling high then diving down and sweeping majestically across the garden as he belched flame after flame at each man in turn until they were all burning brightly, even as they spun around trying to extinguish the flames.

I turned at the sound of a shotgun and found Mrs. O'Donnell, now Shae, and Job pumping their weapons then firing into the heads of the men as they burned.

"Run!" I shouted, as Tyr came in low again, lost to the bloodlust, unable to stop until his enemies were ash.

They nodded, and flung themselves into the bushes as Tyr roared past on his final pass of destruction. Tyr let loose with a veritable torrent of flame that incinerated the bodies entirely, burned away the snow and grass, and sent a shower of earth erupting at least twenty feet into the air.

The once-tiny wyrmling circled the garden, glided down, and landed precariously on the shoulders of the troll then folded his wings. His tail hung almost to the ground as his claws gripped the rock tightly. My immortal friend's long neck craned out as he turned his head from side to side, searching for survivors.

Our eyes locked. I nodded my thanks. Tyr blinked, then promptly fell off the troll and landed in a steaming, hissing heap at the troll's feet.

"Fuckers," said Job as he stomped forward with Mrs. O'Donnell beside him. They stared down at Tyr as he spasmed and squirmed. Job spat on the pile of ash to his right.

"Are you okay?" asked Shae.

"Me? Yeah, I'm fine. At least I think I am. Thanks for coming. Sorry about the noise. Damn, what a mess."

I turned to Phage and covered her with my coat after helping her shakily to her feet. She was shivering and very pale. This was too much, too soon. Shock was setting in. Didn't matter how tough you were, when you think your child is in danger it does funny things to your head. I wasn't feeling so great myself. My system swam with relief, and I almost lost my balance, but Job steadied me and looked into my eyes and said, "You're going to be okay."

I nodded my thanks.

We stood there for a minute or two as Tyr completed yet another change. It wasn't like the others, nothing as dramatic, because he hadn't actually fed. But the bloodlust must have done something to fire up the dragon's juices, because he was truly a creature of terror now. He definitely needed a bigger barn, too. He wouldn't even fit through the doorway now.

"Mrs. O'Donnell, thank you."

"Shae, remember?" she said.

"Huh?" Job did a double take. "You're Mrs. O'Donnell? Haha, you mean her daughter or something, right? Damn, you're hot."

"And you are a smooth talker," purred Shae. They smiled at each other.

I groaned. This was all I needed. These two mooning over each other. But what could she possibly see in him? I wondered. Then the world went black and I clung to Job as I lost my vision momentarily and all energy seeped from me on this cold winter's day in the ruin of my garden.

Phage just stared blankly at the scorched earth.

"So much death," she murmured. "Will it never end?"

"Nope," said Job cheerily. "Welcome to the life of a Necro." Shae punched him on the arm. "What?" he asked.

"Come on, let's get you both inside," said Shae. She took Phage's arm and helped her up the garden towards the house.

"She's a looker. Been keeping secrets from me?" asked Job, following Shae with his eyes, and maybe getting a nice look at Phage's muddy bum.

"It's a long story," I sighed.

"Ain't it always? So, what's with these guys?"

"Just some lowlifes looking to cash in on the animals. And, um, yeah, this sleeping fool is Tyr. Um, he's a dragon."

"Soph, I'm a Necro and your neighbor. You really think I didn't know you had a dragon?"

"Er, yes, actually."

"Then you're dumber than you look. Hurry up, get into the warm. It's bastard freezing out here." Job scowled at the sky, daring it to snow.

The weather must have had it in for him, as at that very moment a torrent of freezing, fluffy ice came down fast and hard.

The ground hissed as snow covered the pyres of the dead.

We walked away.

Several Surprises

Unseasonable heat beat down on us as we finished planting the final shrubs in the garden. The freshly seeded lawn was growing thick and fast thanks to a combination of high temperatures and regular rainfall.

I rubbed my sweaty brow with the back of a filthy hand, firmed the ground around the camellia with my boot, then stood with a groan. My back ached, my knees kept creaking, I had tennis elbow from so much hedge pruning, my face and forearms were covered in scratches from the hawthorn and the damn roses that refused to stop growing, and if I never saw a spade or watering can again it would still be too soon.

But I was happy.

We'd toiled through the winter once the snow had cleared, we panicked when the entire paddock and even the lawn flooded when we got more rain in a weekend than in an entire winter since records began, but the moment the ground was dry enough we'd flattened the lawn, sown the seed, and got to work on the borders.

There had also been a week of hedge trimming, several days of repairing the fences and gates, and I even replaced the rotten posts and installed new stock-proof fencing down at the bottom where our land joined Job's.

"Good work, everyone." I smiled at Jen and Phage as they put their tools in a pile and slapped mud-encrusted hands against their jeans.

"I think it's finished," said a relieved Phage.

"It looks amazing," said Jen as she scampered around the new lawn. I didn't have the heart to tell her we shouldn't be walking on the new shoots. After all, what point was there if she couldn't use it? If it took a little longer to fill in, so what? I'd rather see her happy than stress over a patch of grass.

Phage and I held hands while we watched her dance from plant to plant, admiring the flowers, peering closely at the bees that seemed to have finally returned to England with a communal buzz of relief.

In fact, according to the news, things were definitely on the up. Bees around the world were in record numbers, same for all manner of insects. The European bird population had doubled in the last decade. Numbers were still down on what was seen as healthy, but the projections for the following year were incredibly promising. It was the same worldwide. The new universal currency, the strict ban on fuel consumption, the tight fishing quotas, the eradication of single-use plastic, not to mention the world actually going dark at night and energy pollution at the lowest levels since the start of the industrial revolution, meant that the planet as a whole was finally on its road to recovery. Oceans were gradually clearing of micro-plastics, although they would take centuries to be truly gone, and ubermarkets refused to stock anything that even remotely seemed wasteful in terms of resources, so the number of companies that went bust was insane.

Choice was severely limited now—no packaging. If you wanted milk, soft drinks, or any form of liquid, you brought your own bottle. It meant there were some real winners. Several manufacturers dominated the market, having huge dispensers in shops large and small, and it wasn't the brands most assumed it would be.

Same for crisps, biscuits, chocolate, yogurt, bacon, tins, anything you could think of. There were a few main players, but most produce was now local. You went to a butchers, or a farmer's market, and you bought what was local and seasonal. Everyone was used to it. Everyone wondered what the hell we'd been thinking in the past. Who needs five hundred cereals? Think of the cost of running so many factories. That much transport. The sheer volume of waste. So inefficient.

There were untold losers. Jobs were lost in the millions, maybe billions. Poverty was rife, people were struggling, but even that had miraculously been turned around in a matter of months once the laws came in that put an end to mass consumerism for good. Or so the powers that be told us.

The world was green. An eco-paradise according to our rulers. Jobs in alternative forms of energy production soared, wages were steady, everyone had their fair share, and with farming returning to much more small scale operations there were jobs for all. Strange how things work out.

Of course, it all seemed too good to be true. And it was. We couldn't go anywhere, do anything, see anyone. Most people still worked from home doing weird, nonsensical stuff online that even they didn't understand the purpose of.

And through it all, there was a growing sense of unease even though we rejoiced in our world finally healing after the madness of a century of unabashed exploitation and ruination.

We weren't being given the whole picture. Something was off. What was really going on? How come the reversal was so sudden? Was it even true? The weather was still out of whack. We still couldn't use our cars. Surely there was a fuel alternative by now? Why hadn't they sorted out the battery situation? Wasn't there a way to make it viable and allow us all to be electric, what with all the new solar, wind, and ocean power the planet was producing?

The world was cleaning up its act, but why? We had devolved from a series of nations with independent rule into almost a totalitarian universal government controlled by a few key players. The same went for laws and for our food. The lack of choice meant several companies dominated entire markets, and there were strong hints that even the few varieties we had were actually all controlled by a handful of megacorps.

Was it all a conspiracy to control us under the guise of being green? Was this all a ploy to take control? To remove our liberties and have us exactly where these secretive organizations wanted us? It wasn't even much of a conspiracy theory. It was now becoming clear this was inarguably what had happened. Yes, everyone was healthier, the air and water were cleaner, the planet was in a better state, but it plain didn't feel right. We were being deceived. We were being kept in the dark. There was a plan behind all this and the theories abounded. What was the end goal?

I didn't know. I just knew it was too hot and I really, like really, craved a steak and proper, quality wine.

But we just tended our land, recovered from the events of the winter, and cocooned ourselves in a bubble of family love while keeping as busy as possible.

Phage took weeks to come back to us. She was lost for a while. Uncommunicative, so lethargic she could hardly walk, and just ate and ate. I had to make visits to the shops every other day to try to keep up, but eventually she returned to her usual self and joined Jen and I in the garden. We rebuilt our life together, as was right.

But the questions never ended. Jen bugged me every single day. She was moody, intolerant, disobedient, and angry like I had never seen her. And it was all our fault. She saw what had happened to her mother. She didn't witness the assault, but she sure as hell lived with the result. Peth had kept her inside while our home was attacked, but she'd struggled. Apparently, Jen was about to morph and it took everything Peth had to keep her from appearing right in the garden. I couldn't even imagine.

They'd heard the shouts, the threats, the gunfire and the arguing. And you couldn't miss the huge towers of flame from our friendly dragon.

Since then, Jen and Tyr had been inseparable. They spent hours together every day. Talking, playing. I got the sneaking suspicion they'd even gone for several covert rides, although I couldn't prove it and both denied it vehemently.

Peth had stayed for a week. It was torture. With an ill wife, an insolent daughter who stomped about the place, an idiot dwarf who wouldn't stay in the basement, and all the animals to tend, not to mention Tyr to deal with, I was rushed off my feet, utterly exhausted, sick to my stomach, and stressed to all hell.

It got better the day Peth left, as we had spent way too much time in each other's company. But I had to hand it to her. She pitched in, helped out a great deal, and we even almost got on. A bit. For five minutes late on a Thursday evening, after three bottles of wine and two bars of crappy chocolate. And a movie. And she was asleep.

And now here we were, out in the blistering spring heat, our toil never complete, but the garden was done and the whole property looked better than it ever had.

"We did an awesome job," I said, as we stood by the sculpture and drank cool homemade lemonade with luxurious ice-cubes tinkling in our glasses.

"Play ball with Woofer?" asked our rather-too-portly pooch.

"Sure, buddy. Where's your ball?"

"Not in Woofer's mouth?" He opened wide and looked at the ground, expecting it to fall out as that's where he liked to keep it when he wasn't eating or talking out loud.

"You silly dog," laughed Jen. "Look, it's over there. Fetch Woofer. Fetch!"

Woofer ran all around the garden looking for his ball. We smiled at his antics and drank our drinks.

"No, there. Look Woofer, look where I'm pointing." Woofer looked at Jen then continued to run around. "Why can't you understand pointing?" she giggled.

"Get ball for Woofer? Where is it?" he asked, forlorn.

"So daft," said Jen, as she hopped over to the ball. Woofer beat her to it and stood there, tail wagging, as he asked, "Jen throw ball for Woofer?"

"Yes. Drop it, okay? Woofer, drop the ball!"

Woofer ran off. With the ball.

"It's great we can play here again," said Jen as she came back over to us.

"Sure is."

"Mum, are you okay?"

"I'm fine. It's so nice to be with you all. Sorry about the last few months. I haven't been myself at all."

"We understand," I told her.

"No, we don't. I don't. You need to tell me. Who were those men? Where had you been? What happened to Tyr? He's so different now. He keeps talking about getting married. To me. And he really needs a new home. He can't fit in and he's getting up to all sorts being outside all the time."

"He hasn't hurt anyone, has he?" I asked in a panic.

"No, nothing like that. But he needs somewhere he can call his own."

"Its my next job. Promise."

"So, what's all this about? It's to do with notes and stuff, isn't it?"

"Jen, honey, we can't tell you. I know you were scared, and I know it was a shock seeing Phage like that, but—"

"You too, Dad. You were a mess. Your face was smashed up, you had a limp, and you'd literally just got out of the hospital. I don't know how you could even handle that."

"Yeah, it hurt a lot, but I soldier on. Your mum's strong too. And she's better now."

"Until next birthday, right? Then you go off on another mysterious trip and come back hurt. What if you get killed?"

"Don't worry about it. We're not going anywhere."

"How can you say that?" Jen stamped her foot and glared at us both. "All those men, at our house. They could have done anything. Did Tyr really burn them all?"

"He did. And they deserved it. They would have hurt us all."

"Dad, in case you've forgotten, they did hurt you. And Mum. They nearly slit her throat. This isn't normal. It's wrong, that's what it is. Wrong. You need to tell me."

"We can't, honey. You can't know yet. We've both told you over and over. You're too young. Please, can we drop it?" Phage held out her hand to Jen but she refused to take it.

"Hey, did I tell you about the big guy here?" I asked Jen.

"What about him?" she snapped.

"He moved. He punched out and, er, he hit this guy. Really hard. His arm stayed out for the rest of the night. You didn't see it, but it was back where it is now in the morning."

"Shut up. You liar!" She was intrigued despite her mood. I didn't blame her though, as whose parents got the shit kicked out of them on such a regular basis? Or ever?

"Honest, he did. And I think he wants to, um, try moving again. And maybe he could tell us his name and how he came to be here."

"I thought you brought him here?" asked Jen. "He's not a real troll, is he? Like a *real* one."

"Yes, he's a *real* troll. He just turned up. He was at the old house, and he followed us here. Don't know how, but he did."

We all studied the big dude. Woofer even came over and inspected him. He grew bored pretty fast and cocked a leg.

"Don't you dare," boomed the voice of a giant. If it was chewing rocks and talking with its mouth full.

We jumped back in shock and stared. Woofer lowered his leg cautiously and stared up at the troll then wagged his tail and asked, "Play ball with Woofer?"

Slowly, and carefully, the troll bent at the waist, lowered his hand to the grass, and retrieved the ball. He stood erect, turned his entire frame to inspect the area, then lobbed the ball casually. It sailed past the chickens, over the zoo and barns, and into the paddock at the far end.

Woofer went tearing after it.

"Um, hello?" said Jen.

"Hello," said the troll.

"That was some throw," I said. "And hey, thank you for helping the other month. That was an impressive punch."

The troll bowed his head. He stared at us all, and then a narrow smile spread across his face. The chiseled head rearranged itself to accommodate the change of facial features, like rocks sliding around in a stream.

"I wanted to help. You were in danger."

"Well, thanks. So, what brings you to these parts? You okay with the weather?" I asked cheerily.

"Soph," chided Phage.

"What?"

"That's not much of a question. Hello, I'm Phage. Why did you come to live with us? Do you like it?"

"Like it very much. Nice. Don't mind the sun. Warms me. Enjoy cold too." He shrugged until his shoulders almost met his ears. "I came because I wished to. Adventure. Like adventure. Needed those like me. Necros."

"You're a Necro too?" asked Jen.

"All creatures of magic are Necros," said Phage. "You know that."

"Kind of," said Jen. "So why are you just hanging around?"

"Waiting for note," he thundered.

"What did you just say?" I asked him.

"Waiting for note."

"What note? Jen, go inside please."

"No, I will not." She turned to the troll. "Hey, mister. Is this a Necronote you're waiting for? What's a Necronote?"

"Trolls get Necronote every troll year. Must go kill other troll. Nearly all gone now. Just a few left."

"Fuck!" I muttered.

"Soph," said Phage.

"Oops, sorry. Didn't mean to swear."

"So you get a Necronote?" asked Jen. "Why do you have to kill someone?"

"Don't know. Note says kill. Have to. Or will be turned to dust. Pulverized, dropped in volcano." He shrugged again. Like he wasn't bothered.

"So you have to fight other trolls?"

"Yes. My time comes soon. Almost here. One hundred human years. One troll year. Almost time for Wonjin to go. Must be victor. Not want to die."

"I can't believe this," said Phage. "Soph, did you know this happened to trolls?"

"No, but then, nobody but us has a troll in their garden. They don't talk to humans, never have. Not that I know of."

"Why have you come to us?" asked Jen, utterly in awe of her new big brother.

"Need Wonjin. Came to help you. Stop Phage being killed. Trolls know. We see. Phage must live so Jen can live. Become what she must."

"What must I become?"

"Become what must."

"What does that mean?"

Wonjin shrugged. "Without Phage, Jen would not survive that night. So Wonjin came. Got ready a little early."

"You sure did get ready early. But thank you, Wonjin. It's an honor to meet you." I nodded my thanks.

"Honor Wonjin's. Great prestige on Wonjin for saving Phage and the Jen. Trolls know many things."

"I bet you do. So, you had that all planned, eh?"

"Yes."

"Okay, why do you get the Necronotes?" asked Jen.

"Not know. Always notes. Since beginning when trolls became sentient, notes there. We have memory of all trolls. All ancestors. But trolls not born. Made. Made by parents. Have their memory and memory of their parents. So many others. Troll live long time. Always notes. Now almost all troll gone. Fight. Die. No new trolls."

"That's so sad. So this is what you do? Mum? Dad? You get a Necronote and you go and fight people and kill them?"

"Yes," I said, knowing this had to end now.

"Yes," agreed Phage. "We have no choice, just like Wonjin. It's either fulfill your note or die."

"Why do you do it? Why don't you say no?" Jen was close to tears. She was panicked and clearly regretted asking. I could see it in her eyes, but this had to be done now.

"You can't. If you say no, you will be killed."

"Well, I won't be doing that! I won't be killing anyone. Wait." Jen held up a hand and figured things out. "Dad, you've killed hundreds and hundreds of people!"

"I have." I hung my head; the shame had never gripped me tighter.

"Haha, you can't be serious? You just can't. You? You wouldn't hurt a fly. I see you with Woofer every day. Even Mr. Wonderful. And all the animals. You're a big softy."

"Jen, I love you and your mother more than life itself. I love the animals, and I love my life with you all. But once a year, when I get my note, I go off and I kill someone. I do it. I hate it, but I do it. Sometimes it spills over to other aspects of life. Like last winter when things went very wrong. That's rare, but it happens. This is what you will have to deal with. I'm sorry, but you will."

"I don't believe you! I don't believe any of you!"

Jen ran off.

Phage went to give chase, but I put a hand to her shoulder and said softly, "Leave her be for a while. She's too angry and confused to listen to us."

"But we just told her we kill people."

"Phage, she already knew. Deep down, we all knew. None of us wanted to admit it, but she's a smart girl and she figured it out. Jen might not have wanted to believe it, probably didn't know the details, but she has known for a while."

"We've been fooling ourselves, haven't we?"

"No. Just trying to protect her. There's a difference. Damn, no, you're right. We stuck our heads in the sand and tried to ignore it. Ugh, what a mess."

"I did wrong?" asked our new friend, Wonjin.

"No, it's not your fault," Phage told him. "You weren't to know. So why have you come to protect our daughter?"

"She must be protected."

"But why? Out of all the Necros in the world, why her?"

"She is the Jen. Hmm." Wonjin lifted a fist and placed it under his chin, deep in thought. "Jenny. Not Jen soon. Different soon."

"Yes, she will have a new name when she turns twenty-one," I told him.

"Good name. Rest now. Build energy for Necronote." Wonjin's body assumed the position he'd been in for years. His eyes closed. He was immobile once more.

We tried to busy ourselves for the next hour, giving Jen some space, but all we did was fret, and wonder if we were being neglectful parents or doing the right thing? Isn't that the same for all parents?

Jen refused to talk to either of us for an entire week. It was the hardest seven days of our lives. She hardly ate, she wouldn't go to school, she stayed in her room most of the time, only leaving to go and be with Tyr. When she finally came back to us, it was one Sunday when Phage was cooking Sunday roast.

"Tyr explained everything. I've decided. I want to begin my training. I mean proper training. I want to stay with Grandma, I want to fly Tyr, I'm going to learn how to whisper, how to morph properly, and I want to find out exactly what I am capable of."

My eleven-year-old daughter stood there, hands on hips, defiant. Her face was flushed, her eyes sparkled, and I had never been so scared in my entire life.

I nodded.

"Do you want gravy?" asked Phage.

"Huh?"

"Gravy. On your dinner," I told her.

"Dad, of course I do." She smiled weakly then came over and pecked me on the cheek. Then she went to Phage, who's back remained turned, and hugged her mother while she poured gravy over her dinner.

Big Reveal

"Hello?" I answered my phone just as I finished my amazing Sunday roast. My wife and daughter glared at me for breaking the cardinal rule of absolutely no tech at the dinner table. I shrugged, as if to say, "What could I do?"

"...What, now?..."

"...Okay, no need to be so rude..."

"...Of course..."

"...All of us?..."

"...Probably sleeping..."

"...If you're sure?..."

"...Fine. Be there in five."

I hung up.

"That was Job. He said to come around. Now. Sounded urgent. He was excited. When is he ever excited? He told me to bring Tyr and the both of you. Dogs optional." I glanced at Woofer. He was vibing the leftover potatoes in the baking tray on the counter, trying to mentally force them to fall his way using Jedi mind tricks he believed he'd mastered after watching Star Wars—the good ones—with Jen every single day over the last week. Which is to say, he hadn't heard a word I'd said. And he didn't get any spuds either.

"Maybe he's going to finally tell us what he's been building," said Phage, keen to lighten the mood, which was about as dark as dark can be.

"Do we have to?" moaned Jen.

She had wolfed her dinner, and it was a great meal and I'd certainly devoured it with gusto, but I felt like a whole chapter of my life had closed now. What would become of my daughter? How could we dissuade her from this path she had chosen? Could we?

"I think we should," I told her. "Job's our neighbor, and I know he can be hard work, but he's there for us when we need him. He showed us that. Come on, let's go see what he wants. Jen?"

"Yeah?"

"I'm sorry. We both are. You have to understand that. We did what we thought was right. We have agonized over this for so long, never wanted you to have the childhood we had. We want you safe. Do you understand that? It's all we want, and we have failed you."

"Of course I understand. I'm sorry too. I realize I've been hard work lately. I might have spoken a bit too rashly. Um, can we talk about it later?" Jen hugged Phage and then me. Maybe she didn't really want to leave us. I hoped not. She couldn't. No way. She was too young.

"Of course we can," said Phage. "But please don't be mad at us any longer. We are so sorry, truly we are. Don't spoil your childhood, Jen. Don't go diving into this madness yet. Wait a while. Stay with us. We'll teach you. We will tell you what we think you should know, but you must have a proper childhood."

"Does that mean I can go on dates? With boys?" she blushed, but smiled shyly.

"No. Never!" I shouted, grinning.

"Dad!"

"Okay, when your mother and I are both dead, then you can go on dates."

"But you told me you'll live for pretty much ever."

"Yes, I hope so."

"Mum," she whined. "Tell Dad."

"Sorry honey, but your father's right. You can go out with boys when we won't be able to worry about you. Which means never."

"So unfair."

I laughed, and told her, "Or when you think you are old enough. You can see boys, but no funny business. And the one rule is that they call on you here, so we can check them out." I turned to Phage and mock-whispered, "Plus, that'll stop her going out with boys for years. No kid's gonna rock up here to suffer my mighty handshake and killer glare. They'll be petrified."

"Ha, you'd be surprised," cackled Jen, pointing a finger at me. "You're out of touch. That's how everyone does it these days. We're the new generation, Dad, and we don't spend our lives on phones. We talk to each other. We ask permission of our parents and go about things in a sensible way."

"Huh? What happened to being reckless and never wanting to see the parents?"

"Right, let's go see what Job's up to," said Phage, smiling.

Whenever there was a break in the weather, and sometimes not, Job toiled away at his mysterious build in his miniature woodland. In early spring, he hoisted up a mishmash of tarps, sheets, and anything else he could scavenge to cover the entire thing. Then he went all out with his banging and his swearing. There was many a day when Jen came into the kitchen asking what this new word or that meant, until it got so ridiculous she ended up wearing mufflers if she wanted to play outside.

Job would give nothing away, just grunted, swore, and drank beer while he swung a hammer near your face and glared.

And now here we were, standing at the base of the trees where he had built his treehouse from hell. Or his watchtower, or his bloody antennae to call the aliens.

"Tyr sleepy."

"You've been sleeping for bloody days, weeks. No, months. I told you not to do much when you're awake because you're growing so fast, but oh no, you have to keep on showing off," I lectured.

Tyr had taken to timing himself, with Jen's help, to see how fast he could fly around Shropshire. They'd also got it into their thick skulls that seeing how high Tyr could fly would be a cool thing. For what reason, I had no idea. But they'd been doing it every day, and according to Tyr he could now get close to the sun. Me thinks the dragon exaggerated somewhat.

"Dad, he's just doing what dragons do," Jen told me.

"What, same as my young daughter? Sleep all the time, eat all the food, and complain?" I ruffled Jen's hair and she pulled a face as she squirmed away. She was still my little girl and always would be.

"When you lot have finished chatting, maybe I can get on?" scowled Job.

"Remember what we discussed?" said Shae with a smile.

"Yeah, sorry." Job actually blushed. I think it was the first time in his life he'd apologized.

Shae smiled at him sweetly and squeezed his hand. He smiled back at her, then glared at everyone because we'd seen him actually being happy.

The fact that Shae and he had hooked up took us all by surprise. Nobody more so than the grumpmeister himself. She was, of course, no longer our old neighbor. She used her regular form now, and after the big fight where they'd worked well together as a team, her and Job had slowly begun to get close. We were gobsmacked by her attraction to him, but she said she knew he had a soft heart underneath the gruff exterior. I knew he did, but still. Seriously? Guess it takes all sorts.

"Play ball with Woofer?" my potato-envying dog asked Shae.

"Maybe later. Job's got something to show us all first."

"Yeah, if you lot will shut up for five bastard seconds." He glanced at Jen. "Um, 'scuse my French.

"So what is it then?" I asked.

"Just wait. Right Soph, you grab that rope over there, but don't pull on it until I say."

I moved to where he directed and gripped the rope. Job took hold of the one by him and said, "When we pull, the tarps will drop down behind the build. Everyone ready?"

We were.

"Okay. On three. One. Two. Three."

I pulled my rope, Job tugged his, and the entire covering dropped down behind the towering...

"No way!" I whispered.

"That's... It's..." stuttered Phage.

"That's so cool. It's amazing." Jen ran over to Job and hugged him tightly.

"You like it?" he asked, beaming. He was clearly full of doubt and maybe even insecurity.

"It's incredible."

"Is big playhouse for cats?" asked Woofer.

"No, Woofer. Can't you tell?" asked Jen. "Tyr, look. Look what Job's done."

Tyr lifted up his sleepy head and stared lethargically at the result of years of work. His eyes darted back and forth, looking from one part to the next of the incredible feat of engineering that stretched higher and higher above the treetops. He inspected every element of it, took his time, standing as he did so, his body elongating, his neck craned forward.

Nobody made a sound.

Eventually, he turned his deadly gaze to Job. "You built for Tyr?"

"I did," he nodded. "I knew Soph would screw up and you'd end up being bloody massive in a few years. I know dragons, and I know they need their own place. A sanctuary. Somewhere that's theirs. Well, this is it, Tyr. This is my gift to you, and to all you. This, Tyr, is your very own lair." A thoroughly embarrassed Job turned to us and asked, "If that's okay with you? I don't want to tread on any toes. But, well, I figured he'd need something proper. Something suitable for a mighty dragon. Haha, I knew you'd fuck up and he'd get bloody huge."

"Language," warned Shae.

"Yeah, sorry. Well, is it okay? It's his for as long as he wants it. No strings. Just a place for him to be a proper dragon. I know it's on my land, but..." Job shrugged. "And anyway, you bunch of bastards are always over here anyway, nicking my flowers."

Jen, Phage, and I smiled like idiots as we all grabbed him and hugged this incredible friend and neighbor.

"It's so awesome. Thank you, thank you, thank you," gushed Jen.

"I still can't believe it," said Phage. "So much work. For years. It's incredible."

"Thank you, Job. So much. It really is a work of art."

Job stood tall and proud, and everyone turned to Tyr.

"Well?" I asked him. "You going to do the honors?"

Tyr nodded mutely, eyes gleaming with anticipation. He spread his wings. Everyone stood back to give him room, and boy did he need it. Thick muscle bunched as he squatted on his hindquarters. His neck stretched out, his spines vibrated, his forequarters tensed as the claws pointed skyward, then he leapt almost halfway up the trees then flapped once and landed on a platform. One of many. He peered down at us over the edge.

The large dragon hopped from one stage to the next. He gripped the trees with his claws easily, like he was a born climber, then shimmied up a section before jumping to another tree and a larger platform. Up and up he went, higher and higher.

From platform to tree to thick branch, then right up to the top where a huge staging area sat in pride of place. Several long and sturdy—some might say over-engineered if it wasn't for the use of a dragon—beams jutted out over the tree-tops at crazy angles, presumably acting as perches for our joyous dragon. After circling the creaking boards, Tyr took to the wing and landed right at the very summit of Job's marvelous creation. A compact crow's nest, forever after known as the dragon's nest, where he could hunker down and hide from the weather or stand tall and watch the world all around for mile upon mile. And then he vanished.

"I think he likes it," I said.

"Job, this is so generous. I don't know what to say," said Phage.

"Its nothing." He shrugged.

Shae kissed him. "I think it's marvelous. You're so clever."

"Gotta have something to fill my time. You know me, I like to keep busy."

I slapped Job on the back. "You did a good thing. A great thing. But come on, how did you know he'd need this? It's incredible, and it's going to make him so happy, but you really figured he'd get this big this fast?"

"Stands to reason. Dragons are smart, very smart, and they know what they want before we do. They do their own thing, but they'll be loyal if you treat them right. I know you, Soph. I know the man you are. I knew Tyr would help you if he could. I'm not saying you'd ask him, I guessed you wouldn't want to, but well, he's a dragon. This is what they do. And besides, now he can keep watch over us all. No bugger's gonna attack us again, right? He'll see them a bloody mile away. Can't say I mind having a fire-breathing, acid spewing guard for my property."

"You don't fool anyone, Job," said Phage. "We all know why you did it." Phage turned to Jen.

"You did this for me, didn't you?"

Job nodded. "Your folks are great people, and they want the best for you. It's hard being a Necro, even one that has all these great animals and a cool place like you, Jen. This is a tough life, the hardest, and I knew you'd find out about what it means to be special soon enough. Figured you'd need a place too, just like Tyr. You know, for when the old folks are driving you nuts." He winked at Jen and she giggled. "It's his, but yours too. For when you're older," he added hurriedly as he caught my eye. "That okay?"

"It is. A safe place. A lair, like you said. So, what shall we call it?" I asked.

"Dragon lair?" suggested Jen.

"Something cooler than that," I told her. "Something super cool."

"Sanctuary," said Job seriously. "It's Tyr's sanctuary, his safe place, away from anyone and everyone when he needs it. But it's our sanctuary too. All of ours. Because up there, he can keep a look out. Ensure we're safe when at home."

"You're so sweet." Shae put an arm around Job's waist. I'd never seen him so uncomfortable in my whole life.

"Sanctuary," said Jen. "Hmm, I like it." Her face brightened as she dashed to Job and squeezed him tight again. The idiot old man grinned sheepishly.

"We can never repay you for such a kind and utterly breathtaking gift," I told him. "Years of work, so much planning, and I can't believe how good it looks."

"Yeah well, you owe me one," he said gruffly.

"Tyr," I shouted. "Your new home is called Sanctuary."

"Tyr like Sanctuary." He soared above the dragon's nest then came down in the field and returned to us in the miniature forest.

"My friend," he said to Job, then he rubbed his bony head carefully against Job's face. Tyr now had to lower his head if he wanted to look us in the eyes, I suddenly realized.

"Friends," Job agreed.

It was a beautiful day. Full of hope, happiness, and friendship. There would be hard times ahead, there would be arguments, stress, constant worry. But I knew one thing for certain, a conviction deep down inside me. Unshakable.

Whatever the Necroverse threw at us, we'd survive. If we were nothing else, the people and animals gathered around on this hot spring day were survivors.

What else could we do but keep on battling? Fighting for the ones we loved, searching for a way to purge our corrupted souls?

A swarm of Necrodrones buzzed overhead.

THE END

Will Tyr ever come down from Sanctuary? Will Woofer find a way to get sausages? Will someone please throw the damn ball for him? And what of Jen? No child should know so much at her age. What will she decide to do? And Soph? Poor, broken yet unbending Soph. What's in store next for him, and will he have to face it alone this time?

Find out, or die trying to, in Kill Switch.

Always keep updated about new notes by joining the team. Get news about sales and new releases first; visit www.alkline.co.uk.

The Usual

Some characters I write come alive in my head more than others. Soph, and the rest of his family, and even the neighbors, feel worryingly real. It's like they're there, on the other side of my own overgrown hedges. And yes, I have the hawthorn and the scratches to prove it.

It's as though they're waiting, calling to me, and I can picture myself walking down my own land and climbing the small motte where a castle once sat in the twelfth century. I clamber up the steep, slippery sides of a small hill my family currently have the honor of calling our own, then sit amongst the nettles and long grass, staring off into the Welsh countryside a mere mile from our home, and I listen to Soph recount these stories to me.

Does that sound strange? Maybe that's really what has happened. It sure feels like it at times.

I can see him. I can sense his angst and his despair. His love. His fear and his sadness. His conviction too. His strength and his refusal to give in. There is no doubt his mind is a mess. Nobody with his life could ever be otherwise. I wonder what I would do in his position. What would any of us do? As he says, it must take a special kind of person to be able to enter a battle to the death and never even consider losing. To not fear death.

Is this the way of the samurai? Is that what Soph is? A modern-day samurai? Or is he like the countless millions who have lost their lives in the wars waged on this planet since time immemorial? I have never fought for my life, never even come close, so it isn't my place to say. I could never feel what he's feeling, and yet, as I write these books, somehow I do. How come? I guess this is why I am a writer.

What has made writing this series so far a very enjoyable, almost hypnotic experience, is the sense that although it's filled with magic and utter mayhem, it's not so far removed from everyday life. After all, people all over the world are battling for their own survival. Fighting in wars, struggling for food, trying to figure out how to get through the day. I am in no way belittling anyone's struggle by writing these stories, and they are, after all, entertainment.

But how far away from disaster are we? We've all seen what can happen when a pandemic hits. Some countries are really struggling. I don't know what the answer is; I don't know what will happen, and yet I get the feeling something momentous is on the horizon. I'm just unsure if it will be good, or very, very bad. Let's face it, there are undoubtedly those out to profit from whatever comes. Will they be thwarted, or will life end up being controlled by megacorps, if it isn't already?

Technology is progressing at such a rate, I have no idea what the world will be like when my eight-year-old son is a grown man with a family of his own. When I think back to when I was becoming a man, how different it was. No mobile phones, no personal computers, certainly no smart phones. Now my son laughs when I tell him there used to be three TV channels and most of them showed no programs during the day time. He can't imagine that. He just presses the Prime button on the remote and watches what he wants—as long as it is deemed suitable.

So what's next? And what will our governments decide is best? What will they actually implement? It's all rather bloody scary. Most agree that something has to be done, but will the extreme measures that are actually needed ever be put into place? Or will it all just slowly fall apart until there is no turning back?

Damn, I'm sounding preachy, and that isn't my intention. I was unaware what kind of world Soph lived in until I began writing. It's just ended up being this way. I'm not trying to convince anyone of anything, or push an agenda, as I have no agenda, don't really understand what is going on, and certainly wouldn't know what to do if I somehow got put in charge.

What would you do? What would you do if you were Soph? How would you protect your family? It's clear he's made mistakes, but that's because he's human. And he's old. He can't always see the obvious, and he isn't the best at holding back and figuring things out. But hey, that's what makes him a cool guy, right?

Okay, I'm rambling, but I've grown accustomed to having a chat after each book now, so hopefully we'll catch up again soon.

Book four is Kill Switch. Guess what it's about?

Stay jiggy,

Al

Printed in Great Britain
by Amazon